TIME OUT FOR PASSION

Todd saw Joy racing across the sand, the white gold of her body glistening as she plunged into the waves. He wanted to swim away from her—she might be Julie's killer—but the exciting curves of her slender body and the hunger in her eyes held him.

"Did you ever make love in the water?" she asked, moving close to him.

Suddenly he grabbed her and they kissed, sinking slowly in a salty embrace. *Forgive me, Julie,* he prayed, as his need for Joy blotted out everything else, *forgive me . . .*

AUTHOR'S PROFILE

Robert Colby was born in New York City, attended a public high school and then went to Mercer Junior College.

During World War II he served with the infantry and saw action in the Marshall and Gilbert Islands, as well as at Saipan and Okinawa.

He was a radio and TV announcer for 15 years with NBC and Mutual in New York and with CBS in Hollywood. Mr. Colby is the author of more than 15 published novels, among them the recent Monarch hits entitled EXECUTIVE WIFE, THE FASTER SHE RUNS and BEAUTIFUL BUT BAD.

A Dramatic Novel

LAMENT FOR JULIE

Robert Colby

Author of EXECUTIVE WIFE

WILDSIDE PRESS

LAMENT FOR JULIE

Chapter 1

A minute before five p.m. he pulled to the curb in front of the Longport *Daily News*. While he waited for Austin Lamar Vollmer, president of the *News* and son of the founder, he took the .45 from his pocket and shoved it under the seat. His face was without emotion, his eyes steady on the glass doors.

It was the last day of June, pleasantly warm, and people moved along the streets of the Virginia town with easy strides and purposeless features, as if nothing as monstrous as death ever had or ever would destroy their complacency.

At five, exactly, Mr. Vollmer appeared on the walk in front of the building and looked around him nervously. He wore a drab brown suit, no hat. His shirt collar was open and his tie slightly askew. He was a plump, middle-sized man in his fifties. He had black hair seeded with gray and wore glasses. He did not have the appearance of a man who had inherited a newspaper and several million dollars. Rather, he gave the impression of being a self-made man, with a face carved from the rock of arrogance—the only softness in him was at the belly.

Mr. Vollmer came over to the car and thrust his jaw in the window. "You Powell?" he asked.

"That's right," the occupant of the car lied.

Mr. Vollmer hesitated. He straightened, a hand on the door. For a few seconds he stood uncertainly, his gaze searching up the street, his eyes darting. Abruptly his expression changed, became decisive.

He gave the car a disdainful glance, opened the door and fell heavily upon the seat. They moved off into traffic. After a few blocks, Powell swung away from Broadway onto a residential street which ran parallel to it toward the outskirts of town.

Mr. Vollmer lighted a cigar and, after stinking up the

7

air with a few giant puffs, said, "I realize you couldn't talk much on the phone, Powell, but I don't like all this goddamn secrecy. What do Lansky and his wife want now? Are they trying to hold me up again? Because, by God, they won't get another cent. They were well taken care of."

"I thought," said the man who called himself Powell, "that the Lanskys never did hold you up. Didn't you make them an offer?"

"Well, sure, but you know what Babbitts of the Lansky sort are like."

"No," said Powell. "What are they like, Mr. Vollmer?"

Vollmer gave him a look, twisted the cigar in his mouth. "You a good friend?"

"I wouldn't say that."

"A shoe clerk in a department store," snorted Vollmer. "Sees his first real money in a lifetime and begins to get grand ideas. Thinks I'll pave all his streets with gold." Vollmer hawked and spat out the window. "Well, there are other ways to take care of Lansky and company."

"There are always ways to take care of things if you have the dollar working for you, eh, Mr. Vollmer?"

"That's right and don't forget it. And who are you, anyway? Don't talk wise with me, mister. Now, what I want to know is what are the Lanskys doing here in the first place? I packed them off and told them to get lost— for keeps."

"They got word there was trouble."

"Trouble? What kind of trouble?"

"Gordon Steadman trouble. He's back."

The cigar came out of Vollmer's mouth abruptly. "Steadman! You mean—? I thought he was at sea—on a submarine."

Powell turned off the main highway onto a narrow blacktop falling away between tight stands of trees to the horizon.

"Submarines surface," he said. "Boats come back to port sooner or later."

"I know, but—well, I expected it, of course. I'm not unprepared. Steadman will find everything quiet and forgotten. He's much too late. Say—where are you

8

headed? They're not staying at some goddamn farm, are they?"

When Powell didn't answer but turned left onto a rutted dirt road—just a dusty tongue soon swallowed in the trees—Vollmer eyed him carefully, tossed the cigar and let his hand creep for the door handle.

"I wouldn't try that, Mr. Vollmer." He wheeled right and braked before a ramshackle shed by a stream. When he cut the motor, the gun was in his hand and Vollmer sat blinking into the barrel, draining color, his face losing character in the slackness of fear.

"Who are you?" he said.

"I think you know that very well by now, Mr. Vollmer. I'm Gordon Steadman."

Vollmer brought out a fresh cigar and tried to look composed. The cigar trembled in his hand. He couldn't seem to find his lighter. He put the cigar back in his pocket. His eyes roved over the surroundings, came back to the gun and flicked up.

"How did you find out?" he said.

Steadman was silent. In truth, he hadn't found out much at all. Except the names of the witnesses and a hint that Vollmer money and Vollmer power were behind their sneaky departure from the town.

"I'll sign a check, you fill it in, Steadman. Any amount."

"There isn't that much money in the world, Vollmer." He swallowed. "Do you realize," he said, fighting the pressure of tears, "who we're talking about? Do you?" He grabbed Vollmer by the throat. "We're talking about my wife. My wife!" he screamed in Vollmer's face.

Vollmer's heavy lips hung open, revealing a great block of teeth, irregular, stained with tobacco. There was about him a sick-sweet smell of perfume poisoned with sweat. He tried to speak but only a gurgle of sound came from him. Steadman released his grip.

"Right out there on that road, just about where we turned, it happened, Vollmer." Steadman spoke more quietly. There was need of control, even now. "And unless I get all the answers, Vollmer, this is where it will happen to you. Right here! A dirty, pompous little swollen

9

bug—crushed. Beaten half to death, finished with a slug in the gut."

"I had nothing to do with it," said Vollmer, rubbing his neck. "You have my word."

"Your word!"

"Anyway," said Vollmer, "it was an accident."

"An accident? I see." Steadman nodded. "A little mishap on a lonely road in the middle of the night. An accident. I see. It's very clear." He was on the edge of breaking again. The picture was filling his mind with weeping horror. Kill, kill, kill! was a thundering march that drummed in his brain.

"Vollmer," he said. "You've got seconds left. That's all. Just seconds."

Vollmer turned slowly, looked out the back window through the trees to the join of dirt road, his head cocked in a listening attitude. When he swung back there was a new set to his jaw—not so much fear in his eyes.

"Did you hear that?" he said. "Sounded to me like a car. Roaming around, searching. What kind of car? A police car. Do you think I would go off alone with a perfect stranger—a man like me? Without letting someone know? I didn't get where I am by being a goddamn idiot. That car was never far behind."

Steadman listened and still heard nothing. "Don't bluff me, Vollmer. You can't bluff a man who has nothing to lose. You think I care what happens to me? You've got just as much time as there is slack in this trigger."

"Of course you care," said Vollmer, leaning forward slightly, his eyes snapping with persuasive confidence. "You care more than you think. Don't let your emotions run wild. Naturally you're crazy with grief. And I'm sorry about your wife, believe me. But you'll get over it. And then life will be sweet. I could sweeten it for you. Otherwise—"

"Otherwise, what?"

"Otherwise, nothing but trouble for you. Big trouble. Listen, son—you're not going to kill me. You're not a killer. You're soft inside. I can see that in your eyes. You won't kill me, but you might beat me senseless. And

10

that's when the trouble begins for you. I carry this town right here in my pocket. In an hour every cop on the beat, every squad car and cycle will be hunting you down—if they don't find us in the next few minutes. Don't fight the odds—play it smart, boy. Smart!"

They stared at each other, Steadman with his hate and sorrow, Vollmer with the conviction of a man who never lost at anything.

Steadman waved the gun. "Get out," he said. "You're a lousy judge of character, Vollmer. Out!"

Doubt crept back into Vollmer's eyes. He hesitated, got out. Steadman pushed him along to the broken-down shed. The door sagged on its hinges. Inside, the sunlight of a fading afternoon slashed obliquely over the dirt floor.

"Down on your knees," said Steadman.

"Please, please!"

"Down!"

He stood for a long moment with the gun at Vollmer's temple. He was acutely aware of bird sounds, the faint scratch of leaves on the shed. "Even if you didn't do it yourself," he said hoarsely, "you're almost as bad. Maybe worse. Your kind makes it possible—makes it almost legal. Now—I want to know who you're protecting. Who did it?"

"I . . . I don't know," said Vollmer, looking up with the face of a man still not quite convinced that he would die.

"Pray," said Steadman. "You've got a few seconds to pray. Let me hear it."

"No!" choked Vollmer.

"Tell me about money and power and how it saves you when a bullet goes through your brain and takes off the back of your head," said Steadman. "Oh, Christ, how I wish you could be here to see yourself." He pulled back the hammer. "Good-bye, Vollmer."

"Wait," said Vollmer. "Wait!"

"I'm waiting." And he would go on waiting. He had lied when he said Vollmer was a lousy judge of character. There might come a time when he would kill. But this wasn't it.

11

He was astonished to see that Vollmer's expression was changing again. First came a wary look, then one of certainty, with just the suggestion of a smug smile.

An arm came around fast under Steadman's chin, lifting, locking against his windpipe. He could feel his eyes bugging, the breath going out of him. A hand took the gun from limp fingers while the smile grew on Vollmer's face. Then the pressure was gone and he turned around.

The tall officer in the tan uniform stood spread-legged, holding the forty-five easily, his own weapon holstered. He had a long heavy-jawed face, craggy and burned red-gold in the chemistry of sun and wind. His big shoulders squared above a frame of lean and tapered hardness all the way to the burnished tan of his boots.

There was neither anger nor tension in the gray-green of his eyes, merely a cool curiosity.

In the background, to the right, a chunky officer held a shotgun at the ready and framed in the doorway was a third officer, just then lowering his service revolver.

Vollmer stood up, brushing himself off deliberately. "You want me to die of heart failure, Marty?" he said pleasantly to the tall one. "Next time, see if you can't arrive about three minutes earlier."

"There won't be any next time, Mr. Vollmer," said Marty. "We didn't wanna lay too close and we lost you at the turn-off. Never figured he'd come in here."

The officer who had been in the doorway approached with handcuffs. "You want him in bracelets, Sheriff?" he asked the one called Marty.

The sheriff nodded, Steadman lifted his wrists on command and felt the cool metal cuffs ratchet tight against his skin.

"Outside, buddy," said the sheriff.

Steadman retraced his steps, heard the clump of feet, the murmur of voices, the sound of speech inaudible. He felt nothing, only a deadness and the understanding that this was the end of a phase, perhaps the end of everything. He didn't care.

He paused in front of his dusty gray Ford, behind which, squat and formidable, sun aglint on chrome of

12

siren, sat the police cruiser with the star insignia of the sheriff.

He stood there and no one paid any attention to him. Vollmer had taken the sheriff aside and was talking in low tones. The other two leaned against the squad car with bored indolence.

Steadman didn't know what to do. He thought maybe he had better walk over to the cruiser and see if they wanted him to get in back. Oh, God! Oh, Christ! What difference did it make? What difference did anything make with Julie gone? Even if he found out who and why and how, would that bring her back?

But in a moment, Vollmer, a new cigar in his mouth, stepped jauntily over to the cruiser and got in back, puffing complacently. The chunky cop put the shotgun in the trunk, slammed it closed and slid behind the wheel. There was the sound of the motor spun to life—the police car backed, halted, shoved ahead.

Steadman saw that Vollmer was resting easy on the cushioned seat, the cigar poised in a stubby hand, the hand being brought to his mouth. Vollmer's gaze was on the road beyond the windshield.

And, as the car departed, he never so much as turned his head.

The sheriff opened the back door to the Ford. "Inside, mister," he said.

Steadman ducked and fell limply into a corner. He felt out of place in the back seat. He couldn't ever remember being there except to clean—he and Julie, each with a whisk broom, dusting the shabby interior. Such a little thought—and yet it was a giant of oppression, crushing him.

The sheriff, standing by the front fender, out of earshot, conferred a moment with the other officer. The latter nodded and got behind the wheel, the sheriff climbed in back with Steadman.

The officer fumbled a second or two with the keys, studying the unfamiliar arrangement of the panel. He ground the starter and backed jerkily onto the dusty, pitted road. They jogged away. No one spoke.

The sheriff adjusted his holster, lit a cigarette, extended

13

the pack towards Steadman, straight-arm, not looking at him. When Steadman continued to gaze at the manacled hands in his lap, the sheriff put the pack back in his pocket.

They bounded through the trees to the blacktop, wheeled right toward town.

After a while, Steadman turned slowly and began to study the long rib of the sheriff's jaw, the bronze wrinkles at the corner of his eye, the firm slash of his wide mouth, seen obliquely.

"Sheriff," he said in a tight thin voice, "this is the same road, the very same one. You're the law here. What happened to her? What happened to my wife?"

The sheriff smoked in silence, looking out the window.

"Now goddamnit, Sheriff, don't give me that treatment. Right now, at home, you've got a wife waiting—haven't you? Listen to me. Listen, listen! Haven't you? Haven't you?"

"Shut up," said the sheriff without turning his head. "Just shut up, mister."

In a while they were close to town, seemingly skirting it through side streets. Steadman looked for a police building, a jail. He saw neither. It was not that sort of district—a residential section. He wondered.

The town was hardly familiar to him. In that time before, he had been here only a matter of days. But now he began to have the impression that he remembered streets. Yes—there was the little drugstore where they sold ten-cent sodas, Saturday only—and he and Julie . . . That was what? About three blocks from the house? Sure it was. Another block and they pulled to the curb.

"What're we doing here?" asked Steadman.

"Shut up," said the sheriff.

They waited another minute or two and then the sheriff's car, minus Vollmer, but with the same chunky driver, eased to the curb just ahead.

"Now," said the sheriff, turning at last, "my name is Gifford—two f's as in sheriff. And if you want to get to know me a lot better, just keep it up, mister, just keep it up. You'll wish you never heard of me or the town of Longport, Virginia. You'll wish you were in that tin can at the bottom of the ocean, safe with the rest of the sardines. So you go on to your hut down the street and you pack your junk and get out of here while you can. Because, I wanna tell you, mister, you're the luckiest goddamn fool who ever crossed with Austin Lamar Vollmer since this town heard the name. Now beat it!"

Sheriff Gifford unlocked the cuffs and Steadman got out quietly, went around to the driver's side, replaced the officer at the wheel. But when the sheriff had left the car and was standing, hands on hips, waiting, Steadman leaned out the window.

"Give Vollmer a message for me, Sheriff. Tell him it only takes one man to blow up a fortress if he can find a little hole in the wall. Tell him I've just begun to look for that hole. S'long, Sheriff."

Steadman ground the gears and was gone.

He sat in the rented cottage-size house with its beat-up rented furniture and sipped from the open pint of whiskey. The day closed outside the living room window and interior darkness set him still deeper in the isolation of himself.

Even when he had to grope for the bottle on the table he did not turn on the light. Somehow, though the furniture was scarred and anonymous, it reminded him of Julie, for they had lived here together in the few days before he spent those seven weeks under and over the North Atlantic, entombed in the submarine on which he had been proud to say he was executive officer. And not quite thirty years old.

He held the bottle in his lap now, staring absently at the dull shine of it as it caught a pale swath of light from a street lamp. In that unguarded moment, his mind slid back, skipping the worst of it, holding to unimportant fragments . . .

Another little house, also cottage-size, this one in Hawaii. One of many as they moved from port to port, all alike. If she was there, it didn't seem to matter. She brought her own comfortable atmosphere. She could give a shack personality.

It was a few years back. The boat was operating out of Pearl and they had a one-bedroom at Waikiki, just off the main drag. He came home around ten in the morning

15

after twenty-seven days in the area of the Marshalls. Another exercise.

She wasn't there and he sat down with a lonely beer, watching the door. She came in a half-hour later with a bag of groceries that almost topped the tawny crest of her head. She didn't see him until she was almost to the chair and then she was so surprised, the groceries slipped from her grasp and spewed out onto the floor.

The grin got started on his face and wouldn't stop. He leaped up and grabbed her in his arms.

"Darling!" she gasped. "Oh, darling, when did you——?"

But her words got swallowed in the hungry press of his lips over her mouth. Everything was forgotten in the search of his hands over her body, exploring, discovering her again. For, always, after the long separation, they were like lovers joined in their first affair—yet more violent lovers because shyness was gone, intimacy established.

She pressed toward him, their bodies melding, her tongue darting, entwining, her taut breasts heaving against his chest.

At last she broke away and said, "Oh, God! Oh, sweetheart! This could become downright involved before I even get to know you!"

They laughed. "Well, don't just stand there," he said. "Get to know me!" She giggled and he held her away from him, studying her, matching memory with reality. "You've gained a little, honey. Just a little. But I like it. I really do. You've put it on in the right places."

"You're trying to tell me something," she teased. "That I'm top heavy?"

"I'm trying to tell you that whatever you've done with those extensions under that blouse, it's an improvement. Keep up the good work."

"You fool, you lovable idiot!"

"But here I thought you were wasting away for me and I find you positively ripe and voluptuous."

"Oh, hell," she sighed. "That's only because while you're away there isn't another damn thing to do but eat —trying to feed the real hunger, the one that won't go away."

"Oh, baby," he moaned, kissing her again. "It's so good to be with you, so good, so good."

"I love you," she said. "Lord, how I love you! And now, because I love you, I'm going to feed you. Sit down there in that chair and I'll make you an enormous breakfast. While you eat, we'll talk and talk and talk."

"Eat!" he groaned. "I couldn't even swallow a marshmallow. Not yet, baby. I'm too excited. Talk, yes. By the volume. Later. But right now—"

"Oh-oh," she said. "I see that look!" She made a pretense of crouching to run.

He scooped her up and, nearly stumbling over the litter of groceries, carried her into the bedroom.

He had peeled down to his shorts, was sitting on the edge of the bed, watching her. Slowly she had taken off the blouse and skirt, the slip. And now she stood in panties and bra, combing her long hair before the mirror.

"What is this, a strip-tease and hair-do contest?" He chuckled, trying to hide his wild impatience.

"Don't you want me to look beautiful for you, darling?"

"Yeah, sure, hon. But don't make it a four-star production, huh."

In the mirror she gave him a saucy smile and continued combing her hair.

He saw that she was playing with him, needling his desire. So he gave a huge yawn, saying, "Listen, you got a newspaper around, hon? Locked up in that can, I haven't heard any news in weeks. Just the quickie junk that comes into the radio room."

She turned slowly, gaping her surprise. "Don't you want me, darling?"

"Sure, sure. Plenty of time."

She put down the comb and came toward him unfastening her bra, slipping her shoulders from the straps. Her breasts, unconfined, tremulous, reached outward. They dipped sweetly, rose impudently to urgent nipples. She moved in close until she stood just above him. Then she slithered out of the panties.

He stared now with a fascination he couldn't conceal.

"Oh, God, oh, Jesus, but you're beautiful," he said.

17

"You lie on your bunk, close your eyes and think you remember, but you don't. You don't half remember."

He reached out and pulled her to him, kissed the small mound of her tummy, moved upward to her breasts, shoulders, mouth.

She stepped back with a challenging little smile. She stood naked for one breathless moment before she fell on top of him and they rolled in a tight embrace to the center of the bed.

"Take me, take me!" she whimpered. "Make it all up to me. Make it like you were never gone!"

Then they were locked together. And he was kissing her eyes, her ears and mouth. And they said soft tender things and things violently erotic, all disjointedly spoken in the frenzy of a new-old passion and longing. Until there were no words at all but only animal sounds of ecstasy in that final rocketing release that washes the mind of all but sensation.

He lit cigarettes and for a time they lay side by side smoking in thoughtful silence, a known closeness without need of words.

"It's no good," he said then. "No good without you, baby. You're my whole goddamn world, the rest is garbage. Garbage! Crammed into that sub for weeks on end, thinking, thinking. I get so goddamn lonely for you I could damn near cry. And no one to tell it to, not the way I really feel it. Sure, there are guys on the boat who don't mind it too much, even some of the married ones. But they don't have it for each other the way we do. You can tell, you know? I can think of one or two jokers who're glad to get away, brag about it. Imagine! Not me, buddy. Can't wait to get home, then don't ever want to leave again."

"Don't," she pleaded softly. "Don't leave again, darling."

"Maybe I won't," he said. "I've been thinking about it, mulling it over the whole time." He propped himself on one elbow and looked down upon her, watched the smoke eddy from her soft-rich mouth, loving the way her hair fell in a long burnished tangle across the pillow. "Listen," he said. "I'm going to resign my commission. I've made up my mind. Just now. Just this very second!"

LAMENT FOR JULIE

"Oh, angel, will you? Will you?"

"Why not? I don't have any special talents but I'll take some kind of a job. Anything to get started. Anything that'll keep us together."

"And I'll go to work typing," she said excitedly. "I can do that. I might even qualify as a secretary. Oh, Lord, I'd even scrub floors to have you home. Honest to God, I would!"

"The hell you would! You're not going to work at all, if I can help it. We've got a little dough saved. We'll get along."

He kissed her tenderly. "Julie, I love you. I need you, baby. Too much to go on like this. It's not simple, but if I can arrange it, I'm home to stay. If not, next time out is the last. You'll see."

"Where is home?" she said. "We move like gypsies from place to place. Where is home, darling?"

"Wherever you are, hon. I mean it. The rest is just furniture and a roof to keep the rain out."

She mashed her cigarette quickly and turned into his arms. "You always, always say the right thing. Oh, I'm so happy!"

For moments they clung to each other in silence.

"Darling?"

"Un-huh."

"Now can I have a baby?"

"Sure you can have a baby. Haven't I always wanted it? Have two, they're small."

She giggled. "Oh, I'm practically bursting with love and excitement and—listen, I'm hungry. Are you?"

"I'm starved!"

"Let's eat, then. And drink and make love and talk and start all over again."

"Right! The whole goddamn week-end. Just the two of us."

"It's a celebration," she said. "Because you're not going to leave me again, it's the biggest celebration of my life!"

Chapter 2

They had not moved from the house for two days and he was really hungry for the first time and they ate much and drank a little, talked incessantly, read shoulder to shoulder, slept in a huddle and made love as if they had just discovered it.

As he left for the base on Monday, he swore that he would resign if they had to eat coconuts. But he never did. And there was no child. Not then. But there was one on the way when he came back to Virginia from what was to be the final voyage.

The child was only four months along, dead in her belly, when they buried her.

He swallowed the last of the whiskey in a single gulp and hurled the bottle across the room. Miraculously it struck a chair and didn't break, but fell to the carpet with a dull thud. He wanted to be drunk and he couldn't feel anything but a soggy depression.

He listened inside himself and heard her voice. Bits of conversation, teasing inflections, laughter that began with a giggle and became a squeal. And even a tight choking sob, the end of some argument, for he was easily touched by her tears.

His thoughts drifted here and there and inevitably caught up with the days just past.

One of the cruelest aspects of the whole wretched business was that if there ever was a message sent, and now he doubted it, he never got it. Nothing but a few stale letters when he reached port. And his phone call unanswered, though he wasn't worried because he supposed she was in town shopping or visiting some neighbor.

He had taken a taxi, riding over the unfamiliar streets, carrying inside of him the big excitement and the big love which he had been building and storing the whole seven weeks.

20

LAMENT FOR JULIE

He went surging up the walk, only to find the door locked, no answer to his ring, the house having a strangely vacant aura about it.

So he had gone next door and the thin pale woman with the blotchy skin dried her hands on a dish towel, eyed his uniform curiously and gave him the oddest look when he asked where he could find Mrs. Steadman. It was a look which said the question was so absurd, he was to be pitied.

"Well," she said, "I see you're in uniform so I suppose you're a friend of the husband. But, heavens, I thought everyone knew because it was in all the papers. The poor girl is dead, you know."

He had a distorted image of himself from there on. Somehow, he was shaking the woman by the shoulders and begging her not to say that, not to dare ever say that again. Never! And, of course, she was terribly frightened of him, but when she got it straight who he was, she began to cry, unfolding the story in disjointed bits of horror, gulping it out in tearful spasms, pausing to insert that dreadful phrase over and over—*You poor man, you poor dear man . . .*

And then he ran, stumbling, hurling himself at the house, crashing his fist through a pane, getting the window up, racing around the empty rooms shouting, *Julie, Julie, Julie . . . !*

But it was all done, and what was done . . . And she was buried, her mother having long departed after attending to the arrangements. And the faces in the district attorney's office were blank, their words about inconclusive evidence, impossible grounds for a case without witnesses adding up to a trail covered by sand drifts of corruption swept down from high places. And Julie Steadman just a name in a file.

He had understood quickly the uselessness of an open battle and, planning in secret, he had gone underground for the truth. But truth was a joke because there was no one to uphold it.

The only justice was his own.

He had nosed around, using the name Powell because he had found that his own name brought only guarded looks and cautious answers. He had located a bitter ex-cop by the name of Floyd Whitlock and from Whitlock he had learned just enough about the Lansky couple to guess that they had once identified the car as one belonging to the Vollmer clan—before they suddenly withdrew as witnesses and left town.

He had thought to frighten the rest out of Vollmer himself. It had almost worked. Another minute and he might have known. But he had failed and now, in spite of his brave talk, the odds against him were too overwhelming. He needed help. From someone who was a total stranger to this town. A man who could move about with freedom, disguising his purpose.

Todd Corwin would come on the run. Todd had always been crazy about Julie, in a platonic way, of course. Todd was with him in the sub service for a time, until his father had died and left him a couple of good-sized cruise ships, double-deckers with which his father had made a fine living taking the tourists on excursions through the Florida Everglades.

Even though he hadn't seen Todd for a whole year and hardly a letter had passed between them, Todd was still his best friend. Whenever they got together their closeness was so quickly renewed it was as if no more than a day had passed. Todd did not make subsurface friendships casually but when he formed a bond, his loyalty, though unspoken, was fierce.

Todd was one big hunk of man, physically and spiritually. At thirty-four, he was six-two and underweight at two hundred, though you could lay a ruler flat across the hard fiber of his belly. In the simplest kind of physical exertion there was pleasure in watching him, for all his movements sang of grace and rhythm and easy power, like a great oiled machine merely idling, its reserves untapped.

Yet he was no exhibitionary muscle-man in appearance or action. He talked sparingly and often with a bitter humor to cover a massive gentleness and sensitivity. His hair was soft-blond and unruly. His face was inclined to fullness, the nose small, the mouth wide. His eyes were quiet gray-blue and probingly watchful.

He took almost anyone but himself seriously and it was nearly impossible to prod him to superficial anger.

LAMENT FOR JULIE

But once deeply aroused, nothing could turn him off. He was a deliberate and calculating enemy.

Todd Corwin was perfect for this kind of hunt and vendetta and Steadman had only kept silence until now because Todd was the one man to whom he could not say, *Julie is dead* and keep his voice flat and impersonal. And once spoken to Corwin the words would no longer be words, but fact.

Steadman put on a light, found the phone and dragging the cord behind it, returned to his chair. He dialed the operator, then doused the light again. He gave the Florida number and waited. Todd was a bachelor and Gordon expected he'd be out—having dinner with one of the several gals on his current roster. But, surprisingly, in less than a minute, his voice was filling the line.

Steadman fumbled the conversation for a few seconds until Todd said, "Something wrong, Gordy? You don't sound good. Julie all right?"

"Julie?"

"Of course, Julie. What the hell's the matter? You two have a fight? Or are you loaded?"

"Oh, Christ, I wish I *could* get loaded. Listen, Todd. Are you listening?"

"I'm listening, Gordy."

"Something's happened to Julie."

"My God. What? What?"

"She's gone, Todd. Gone."

"Gone? She left you?"

"Left me? I wish it was that—I wish it was only that. No—Julie's . . . Julie's dead."

"Julie! I don't believe it. C'mon, fella. You're drunk, aren't you? Did you say—?"

"Dead," he gulped. And then he began to weep. And he took the phone away and held his hand over the mouthpiece. While distantly he could hear Todd shouting his name.

After a time he got hold of himself and explained it all in a flat tired voice, as if talking about a stranger.

". . . Of course, they say it was an accident, Todd. Hit-and-run, some drunk, they want me to believe."

"And, naturally, you have reason to think otherwise."

"Every reason. In the first place, what would Julie

23

be doing walking along a lonely country road on the outskirts of town in the middle of the night? You knew Julie. Does that sound like her?"

"Nothing like the Julie I remember. What else, Gordy?"

"The district attorney had a couple of witnesses—man and wife by the name of Lansky. They saw Julie get into a car downtown. An hour or so before it must have happened."

"And they recognized the driver?"

"No, they recognized the car as one of four that belong to Vollmer. I told you, Vollmer practically runs this town, owns the only important newspaper. Vollmer has a wife, a son and a daughter who drive, also a chauffeur. But all the cars are in his own name. His license plates have low numbers—V-1 through V-4. That's important to remember."

"And how did the Lanskys know Julie?"

"They didn't. There was a picture of her in the paper and they recognized her from it. She came out of a late movie the same time they did. They were right behind her when, about two blocks away, she got into this car. The driver was in shadow and they couldn't see who it was. But the car was a red Cadillac convertible and they read the number V-3 on the license plate—never thought anything more about it until the story broke."

"Then what?"

"They were willing to testify one day. And the next, said they were confused, not at all sure. Then they packed up and left town. Just disappeared. Vollmer paid them off."

"Where did you find all this out, Gordy?"

"From an ex-cop by the name of Whitlock. He was on the case and got fired from the force. He was only guessing that there was a pay-off. But, as I told you, I tricked Vollmer into an admission. Proving it is something else. God Almighty, even if I do get the truth, what good will it do? It won't bring—" his voice broke again, "bring back Julie."

"I know, I know, Gordy. Jesus, I know. I just can't believe that Julie is—oh, the bastard, the evil, murdering bastard who did it. Kill 'im with my bare hands. Gordy?"

"Yes."

"I'm coming up there to give you a hand."

24

LAMENT FOR JULIE

"I was hoping. Todd—"

"I'll call Hugh Kroetz. He can take over for me. Then I'll catch the first plane. I'll be there in the morning, maybe before if I make good connections. And Gordy— we'll have a talk—we'll make plans. But we'll have to meet in secret. I'm no good to you if they're watching me, too. So I'll check into a hotel, then give you a call. And Gordy—you know how I felt about Julie. I can't say how sorry . . .Gordy? You there?"

"Can't—can't talk now, Todd."

"I understand. God love you, fella."

The line was dead. Steadman hung up.

He went into the bedroom and lay down in the dark. Why would Julie accept a ride with a stranger? It was completely out of character. And which one of the Vollmers was it? And why would anyone want to harm her? An obscene picture of her frail body, smashed and torn by the big car, wouldn't go away.

His hand touched the empty space on the double bed where she should be lying beside him. He groped until he found her pillow, buried his head in it. Again he wept.

He couldn't stand it. He couldn't just lie there thinking. He would go out and get another bottle—drink himself into oblivion.

He sat up. He swung his feet off the bed. And then he heard it. Thin, metallic, a key sound. He put on a light and started for the bureau where he kept the forty-five.

He had his hand on the drawer when he remembered they had taken the gun away from him.

Todd Corwin checked the flood of his emotions over the death of Julie Steadman until he had called the ticket office. He made a reservation on the next plane out of Miami to Longport via Washington. Then he brought half a glass of bourbon on the rocks to a chair and slumped down in a stupor.

Julie dead. Julie a wax distortion of herself in a box, the box sealed in the ground. Impossible! Yet Gordy's weeping voice on the phone hadn't lied. And Corwin wanted to weep himself. For there was a time when he had also been in love with Julie. And though the pain of losing her to Gordy had diminished in the years which followed, he had never stopped loving her. He had only pushed the knowledge of it down into that storeroom of the subconscious where the wounds and disappointments of life lay hidden. And because his inviolate friendship for Gordy was not restricted by mean jealousy and bitterness, he had readjusted. He had allowed his relationship with both the Steadmans to mellow and ripen into a strong bond of unspoiled affection.

Yet now, at Julie's death, there was a certain release from the suppression of old longings. Since Julie did not exist except as a memory, he could examine plaintively the truth of his feeling for her as it must always have been from the beginning.

He and Gordy had both been in the sub service together. For a period they had even been on the same boat. During this period the boat would occasionally tie up at Port Everglades on the east coast of Florida, north of Miami. Todd lived nearby and he would take Gordy home with him and arrange a double date. Or, if there were other navy vessels in port, the Chamber of Commerce would hold a dance for officers. Todd liked to go to these dances because they were always fed by a fresh crop of carefully selected, unescorted gals—seldom a real dog in the bunch. Todd was bored with the same old talent around home and welcomed the change.

It was at one of these dances that they met Julie. She lived in the area, had gone to the dance reluctantly, urged by a girl friend. They had both danced with Julie frequently during the evening, both had asked to see her again. She had gone out with Gordy the following night, Todd the next. This had continued for several days until it was a kind of joke between them. Each would admit no more than a passing interest.

Actually, Todd could not estimate Gordy's feelings exactly. He did not know Gordy quite as well as he came to know him later. And Gordy was shy about putting emotions into words. But there was a clue. For once, Gordy did not seem to push the idea of a double date. So, if he wanted to be alone with her . . . Well, it was pure speculation.

Meanwhile, Todd was falling in love with Julie and didn't know quite what the hell to do about it under the circumstances. He didn't want to strain his most valuable friendship. But he couldn't get Gordy to admit any more than that Julie was "fun to go out with, a lot of kicks, that's all."

The problem solved itself. Temporarily. Orders came, they put out to sea. On that morning, Todd phoned Julie.

"We're pulling out," he said. "I don't know just when we'll be back. I expected to see you again tonight. But now—Julie, I've got to say it or I won't sleep a wink. Julie, I love you. My God, it sounds so flat and empty on the phone. I'm here in this damn stuffy booth with the sun outside making a fool of me. But, Julie, there it is, I love you!"

"Oh, Todd, Todd. You're so sweet. I don't know what to say, I really don't."

"Repeat after me, I love you, Todd."

"That would be nice, if I was sure, Todd. It's just the wrong time anyway. I think you're a wonderful guy. But about the other, let's talk about it when I see you again."

"Julie?"

"Yes?"

"Gordy is a very good friend. The best. But he won't speak his mind and I can't read it. Has he said anything to you?"

"You mean about—? No. No, he hasn't, Todd. Not a word that you could call serious. Anyhow, don't worry. I wouldn't come between you."

"Well, Gordy is not exactly the aggressive type. But what about *your* feelings?"

"I don't want to talk about my feelings. It's much too soon. Got to go now, Todd. Call me. Don't forget."

"Listen, how could I forget? 'Bye, Julie."

They returned in a few weeks, each saw Julie, and still nothing had been resolved.

Then Gordy was transferred as exec on another boat. Todd's father died, he resigned his commission to take over the sight-seeing boats his father left him, and all at once had Julie to himself. He felt a little guilty, but also ecstatic.

He saw Julie three or four times a week. They swam, played tennis, danced. And in a very minor sense, made

27

love. One way or another she dodged all his attempts to discuss marriage or his love for her. Until one night he sat her in a corner at a small dim bar and made her listen to all of it.

"All right," she said after a thoughtful silence. "I'm going to be terribly honest. I hoped there might be something for us, Todd. I really did. But while I need you and hate to let you go, it just isn't there."

He nodded solemnly. "Well, at least that's the truth and I can stop beating myself to death. Is there someone else?"

Her face went through the changes of indecision. She bit her lip, frowned. "Yes," she answered. "There's Gordy."

"I see. I see—Well, good, good! But why didn't you say so before?"

"Because—because he keeps writing me but he never tells me he cares. He hints. Oh, he hints, all right. But you can't live on a hint. Oh, Todd, Todd, I don't want to hurt you. And I didn't want to admit it even to myself. But I think I loved Gordy almost from the first night we were together."

"You're both a couple of dopes," he said, turning away. "I'll write him tomorrow."

"No! Please don't do that. I'd die. I'd just die if you told him."

"Okay, I won't. But on one condition. You write him the truth yourself. First thing in the morning."

Well, she did write him and they did get together and there was a marriage. For him it was a sad-happy affair. And then he dropped one kind of love into the well of his mind and dredged up another.

But now he couldn't help remembering again the feel of her in his arms, the moist warm touch of her lips, the husky kindness in her voice which he had once mistaken for love. There were fragmentary images of her in various attitudes and places. Something like a hundred nights, a thousand laughs and a million words shared. All for nothing.

Julie, Julie, he thought. *Dear, dead Julie. My God, what happened to you? What did they do to you?*

And then, because there was still too much thinking

28

time before the plane, and more violent emotions than could be contained without action, he stormed into the bedroom and began to pack furiously.

In his room at the Longport Plaza Hotel, Todd Corwin gave the operator Gordy Steadman's number and looked at his watch. It was twenty minutes before seven a.m. Darkness was already being sucked out of the sky by a mounting sun when his plane touched ground. There had been a delay in Washington before he caught a flight to Longport. While he waited he had called Gordy several times and got no answer. For a man in Gordy's state there were a number of possible explanations. He didn't like any of them. He was worried.

They were ringing now. The buzzing went on in his ear—three—four—five—

"Yeah?" The voice didn't belong to Gordy.

"Who's this?"

"Same question, Mac. Who're you?"

"Must have the wrong number. I want Gordon Stead-man."

"You got the right number. He can't come to the phone. I'll give 'im a message."

"Thanks a lot. I'll tell him myself."

Corwin pressed his thumb down on the disconnect bar. Frowning, he held it there, then released it. He ordered a taxi and told the operator he would be watching for it at the main entrance.

He crossed the room and looked at himself in the mirror. His clothes were rumpled, he needed a shave. That could wait. No sleep and he should be worn down. He wasn't. He was never so alert, never coiled so tight within himself.

He opened the suitcase at the foot of the bed, lifted clothing, found the .32 automatic. He checked the clip, shoved it back into the butt. For a moment he weighed the gun in the palm of his hand, wondering if he needed it. With a shrug, he tossed it back into the case and shut the lid, locking it with the small key.

He went out to the elevator, pressed the button savagely. When the lift didn't come immediately, he raced down the stairs to the street.

Corwin got the whole picture, the end result, a block away. He sat heart-frozen on the edge of his seat while the fact settled dead-weight in his mind. While the cab gained on the police cars, the ambulance, the wad of hungry-faced people in front of the house.

"Drive on, drive on!" he told the cabbie. "Let me off in the next block."

He returned casually, walking in long slow strides, loosening his face muscles. The sun was already hot on his back and yet in the ribbon of his spine he felt a gigantic shiver.

The two cops were holding the crowd on the walk, pressing them back from the house. A pale slim man held a small boy on his shoulders. The child's mouth hung open around a lollypop, his eyes wide with the bright wonder of this strange circus.

Corwin wanted to charge through from the rear, ram flesh aside, snarling, shouting. Instead he wedged and squeezed, moving carefully forward, the mass giving way to the hard thrust of his big shoulders. Faces turned upon him with scowls of annoyance which fled at the look of him, while barbed tongues went silent. It was as if there could be felt about him some inexorable force which made their own wills puny and ineffectual.

"What's up, Officer?" Corwin made it sound impersonal, afraid his face might be giving him away.

The officer, straddling the walk, hands on hips, gave him a long appraisal. "Shooting," he said. "Guy knocked himself off."

"That right?" Corwin said. The shiver which had been threatening broke over him and his fingers spasmed, balled into fists. "Why would he do that—knock himself off?" His voice stumbled on the words and when the officer looked at him sharply, he formed his lips into a smile.

The officer shoved his cap up and mopped his brow with a big square of handkerchief. "I only know what I hear, bud. The man's wife got creamed by a car—some hit-run bastard. Guess he blew his top—with a gun."

"With a gun? What sort of gun?"

"What's the difference? When you're dead, you're dead, even if it was one of the B.-B. rifles."

30

"Oh, it was a rifle, then?"

"Jesus, you ask a lot of questions. Nope, it was a chop-nose .38 and, brother—Hey! Hey, you there! Move back, move back! My God, these yokels would buy tickets if we'd let 'em in."

"Sure, sure," said Corwin. "Did they uh . . . did they remove the uh—"

"Nope. The bloody thing is still in there. Why do you think these jerks are standin' around? They're waitin' for dessert. But take my advice and go home, mister. You won't see nothin'."

He didn't want to stay. The thought revolted him. But he did. It was the sort of thing you had to do—a feeble kind of homage. He watched the shrouded form all the way to the ambulance, watched the door close, the vehicle roll off down the street. He shed no tears, his face showed nothing, though he was soggy-sad inside and the moan was just behind his lips.

When the ambulance was gone he walked on up the street, hating the few who still gawked and gawked at the house. His mind centered on the gun—the chop-nose .38, as the officer called it. That was important. Because he was certain that Gordy never owned anything but a .45 as long as he had known him. Otherwise, he would have believed it—that Gordy blew himself out of a world he couldn't face without Julie.

He began to walk faster, looking for a cab, a bus, any kind of transportation. He was in a hurry. He would always be in a hurry. Until he found out about Julie. Until he caught up with whoever it was that murdered Gordy Steadman.

Chapter 3

"No," said Floyd Whitlock emphatically. "I don't give a damn if he was your own brother. I can't help you, Corwin."

"Can't?" said Corwin.

31

LAMENT FOR JULIE

"Can't and won't," Whitlock answered. He was a bulky man not far from fifty, bald except for a few loose strands of yellow-brown hair. He had puffy cheeks, black eyes in deep sockets. Words gushed out of him rapid-fire, as though pushed to catch up with the angry turmoil of his mind. His hands were busy kneading the arms of his chair. He seemed to scowl perpetually.

He lived in a small ground-floor apartment on a shoddy side street west of town. His wife, he told Todd, worked as a court stenographer—he had a daughter in high school.

Corwin had found the address in the phone book and, after cleaning up at the hotel, he had rented a car, driving numbly out to Whitlock's place with the urgency to keep on the move before he became enveloped by a giant crush of melancholy.

It was just past eleven—Gordy's body had been in the morgue less than four hours.

"Look," Corwin said, "when you took this case there was one murder—now there's two. You should be twice as ready to help."

"I'm not on this case, remember?" said Whitlock. "I was fired. I'm not a homicide detective any more. I'm not even a foot patrolman. I'm not a cop. Period! I'm a private citizen and I'm not interested."

"You were a private citizen when you talked to Gordy Steadman about his wife." Corwin leaned forward, aiming a finger. "And even a private citizen is interested in murder—if he knows something about it."

"What murder?" Whitlock picked a magazine off the table at his elbow and began idly to roll it tight. "A woman is killed in a hit-run and her husband shoots himself. That's murder?" The magazine became a club with which Whitlock slowly beat the palm of his hand.

"All right," said Corwin, getting up, wanting to take Whitlock and the whole town apart with his bare hands. "I won't waste my time. Did they buy you off, or scare you off, Whitlock?"

"I'm not for sale!" Whitlock shouted. He hurled the magazine across the room. "But I know when to scare. I've been in this goddamn town long enough to know who deals the cards and from what part of the deck, mister.

32

LAMENT FOR JULIE

I've got a wife and a kid and no job. I've got mortgages and car payments. The bank still owns the stove, the refrigerator and half the furniture, too. You know where I'll wind up? If I'm lucky—night watchman at forty per."

"I agree. You probably will," said Corwin quietly. "But is that so important? You'll make out. And when you come home from the job, you'll sleep."

Whitlock waved his arm at the chair. "Oh, sit down, sit down, for God's sake. It's not the job I'm thinking about."

Corwin sat. "Besides, no one's asking you to do anything. All I want is information."

"I gave your friend information," said Whitlock hoarsely. "And what did he do with it? He took it out and killed himself with it. That was the gun that killed him—a little knowledge. You think you'll be any different? You wanna know what's eating me, I'll tell you. As far as I'm concerned, I might as well have pulled the trigger on Steadman myself."

"The trouble with Gordy—" Corwin's voice failed. "The trouble with Gordy," he began again, strongly, "was that he was in a hurry. He went right in the front door. I have other plans."

Whitlock was silent.

"Will you help?"

Whitlock spread his arms. "How can I help? If I buy cigarettes at the corner, that's suspicious. If I go to the john, they know about it."

"What do you know that you didn't tell Steadman?"

"Nothing. Not one goddamn thing."

"What do you guess, then?"

"Same as you. That Steadman had to be kept quiet. He found out too much."

"And Julie, his wife?"

"It could have been an accident Vollmer wanted to cover. But I don't think so."

"Why?"

"According to the Lanskys—I talked to them myself—she came out of a movie and got into a red Caddy belonging to Vollmer. The Lanskys read the plate number—V-3. The car Vollmer generally uses himself has a V-1 plate. The others are V-2 and 4. Anyway, assuming she wasn't a pickup, she had to know the driver. Could've been Vollmer himself, the son or the daughter, the wife or even the chauffeur. Maybe a friend of the family, for all I know. Anyway, she goes off with whoever it was and a couple of hours later she's found squashed on a country road just outside the city limits. She didn't walk out there —she must have been driven in the Caddy. If someone ordered her out of the car, forced her to hike, and she was run over by still another car, then what would Vollmer have to hide? That someone took her for a ride and they had an argument and she got out? Not enough for this kind of stir. Nope. She must have been struck by the Cadillac—on purpose."

"How come this couple—the Lanskys—were able to read the plate and still couldn't tell who was in the car?"

"Simple. The car was in darkness, mostly. But the plate has a light just above it. Clear as daylight. And you don't forget a number like V-3."

"Okay, what did you do that got you fired?"

Whitlock flamed a cigarette and looked through the smoke with narrowed eyes. "After the Lanskys disappeared, I was told to lay off, that the case was closed. High as he is way up there, I could smell Vollmer. I kept at it on the QT. Vollmer's chauffeur caught me snooping around the red convertible in the garage and hopped on the phone."

"Did you find anything?"

"Yup. I think so. There wasn't a scratch on that car. But the paint on the right front fender just missed, for my dough. When they re-paint any portion of an auto, no matter how good the match, that new color is going to be just a wee bit brighter until it wears awhile. Brighter— that's how I could tell. They should've painted the whole car."

"Oh, the bastards, the bastards! Did you check any of the body shops around?"

"Sure. Nothin'. But it could've been done at home by the chauffeur with a little know-how."

"Any idea where I might hunt the Lanskys?"

"None. They could be in the next town or out of the country."

"You don't think they were shut up for good?"

LAMENT FOR JULIE

Whitlock flipped his cigarette into the fireplace across the room. "Unh-uh. I don't think so. Couple of hungry kids—greedy. A thousand would have bought them and I'll bet they got twenty-five or better."

"Anything else, Mr. Whitlock?"

Just some advice. Leave it alone. Go on back home. The whole structure of this town is rotten at the top and it's going to fall on you like it did on the Steadmans. You can't win. So they were friends of yours—damn good friends. They fell into an evil situation—God knows what kind of evil. So what? They're gone and revenge is for dopes. It don't change nothin'. You put out a fire here and another one starts there. It's like those wars to end wars. The first, the second, the third—and then the fourth and the fifth and the sixth. Forget it and go home and live your life, son. That's all. Don't let them send you home in a box."

"That's what you'd do if you were me? Just forget it, huh? You could do that?"

Whitlock offered a small tight smile. "Maybe not. But that's what you should do, just the same. If you've got sense. But I can see you haven't. You've got the look. So where will you start? Why don't you beat up a few people, including Vollmer himself. You might get a confession."

"Oh, no. I realize you're goading me. But just the same, it occurred to me. They understand those methods. What they can see and hear and feel, they can handle. This calls for something subtle and sneaky—friendly, with a knife up the sleeve. Somehow I've got to get close to the Vollmers, get behind their lines of defense, fight in their own camp. Any ideas?"

Whitlock brought out a fresh cigarette, twirled it between thumb and forefinger. "I don't know about Mrs. V., but Vollmer is a bad bet. There's nothin' there to get close to. If that sonofabitch has a heart, they built it for him at some zombie parts factory. Out of cast iron. The boy, Matt Vollmer, he's about twenty-two, just out of school, mean as his Old Man and twice as useless. Give him a bottle, a babe, all the dough in the world and he's happy. Then there's Gail Vollmer. She's about a year older— queer, moody and man-happy. She's the Old Man's favorite—so they say. She can do no wrong. And like her brother, if she don't do wrong, what does she do? Nothin'. From the look of you, I'd say she was your best bet. You're built to interest her and she's built to interest any guy with even one decent male hormone."

"If she's a Vollmer, I'd hate her."

"Naw, you wouldn't. The Old Man is the one to hate. And if you can get close to that Gail, you might just get a lead."

"I wouldn't know where to start."

Whitlock gave light to his cigarette. "Well, let's see. This time of year she'd likely be down at the Surf and Tennis Club, over at Carleton Beach on the ocean. You take the main drag until you hit Carleton Beach Road, then you cut left and follow it right out."

"Hold it, hold it. You're moving too fast. Isn't that a private club?"

"Yup. But I could get you in. I know Charlie Milano, the manager. He has just about the same love for Old Man Vollmer that I do. Vollmer's one of the directors and they've kicked words back and forth at each other a couple of times. Vollmer always won, of course. You want me to call him—Milano?"

"It's worth a try."

"Let's see. You're in the cruise boat business, are you?"

"Right."

"You better have some angle. There's a private anchorage over at Harbor Beach, nearby. Bennett's. They berth yachts and they sell cruisers and a small-boat line. The place is for sale. I heard Bennett wants a hundred and seventy-five thousand. Now, what you wanna do is exaggerate your own business. Maybe you've got a fleet of these cruise ships operating along the south coast of Florida. And you're looking to buy out Bennett's—at a price so low he won't sell. You offer a hundred and forty or fifty maybe. I know he's come down already and won't budge an inch more. But this way you'll be on tap for a reason and you'll be able to stall around."

"Good! I'll have a look at Bennett's later."

"Take off, then. Ask for Charlie Milano at the gate. Meanwhile I'll put in a call and see that you get the run of the club for a few days. But you listen here—once you get in, forget me. You never heard of me. Understand?"

LAMENT FOR JULIE

"Certainly. And thanks a hell of a lot, Mr. Whitlock."

"Floyd is my name. And you keep in touch—by phone. Don't come here again." He stood up. "They haven't finished me yet, and I'm on your side, boy. I still could help underground. Hear?"

Corwin bit his lip. "Oh, the bastards," he said. "The dirty murdering bastards."

En route to the club, Corwin bought himself a pair of swimming trunks, a tennis outfit and sneakers, a racket and a can of tennis balls. It was duplication. At home he had all of these things but he could hardly have anticipated the need to bring them along.

The Surf and Tennis Club was surrounded by a massive stone wall. A wide gate stood open and just beyond the gate was a small booth housing a uniformed attendant. At this booth Corwin paused, said, "I'm looking for Mr. Milano. My name is Corwin."

"Yes, sir, Mr. Corwin. Mr. Milano phoned down you were coming. Find him in the main building, straight up the hill."

Corwin waved and pushed the rented Buick ahead. Beyond, at the top of a rise, he could see what had to be the main building—a long structue of gray stone and glass set behind a welter of trees. Below it, to the left, were two smaller buildings between which could be seen the hedge and fencing of a tennis court.

The parking area to the right of the main building was well seasoned with shiny cars, mostly of late vintage and costly make. Corwin parked at the extreme end, not without a purpose.

He climbed out and, as he made his way through the rows, he let his eyes drift over the license plates. He found it about midway, a cream-colored Lincoln sedan with the number V-4. If not Gail, at least some member of the Vollmer clan was present.

The interior of the building was spacious, immaculate. Cathedral ceilings, the gleam of dark woods, heavy furnishings, more comfortable than regal. Corwin made a quick tour.

Off the foyer to the right, there was a vast lounge with scattered easy chairs before expanses of glass on either side of the room. West, there was the great spread of the grounds and east could be seen a swimming pool in the foreground, while below it, a sweep of beach fell away to the ocean. On the other side of the foyer was a dining room, more glass, more view. East of the dining area Corwin found stairs and followed them down.

He was in a paneled bar. Around most of the room were portholes. Behind each porthole was a small tank. A variety of fish in these tanks swam and nibbled and stared upon the room with piscatorial boredom. In back of the bar, heavy glass dropped all the way from the ceiling. The glass enclosed a section of the swimming pool and the legs of swimmers could be seen churning the water. Occasionally someone dived and, hair streaming, peered in myopically, made a face and departed.

The lighting of the room was murky. The tables were vacant, though several people in tennis togs or bathing suits sat at the bar, chattering noisily. Corwin took a stool a little removed from the others and ordered a drink. When the drink came, he carried it to a corner table and sipped morosely.

Gordy was probably in one of those sliding drawers at the morgue, a great filing cabinet of bodies, a sad little identification tag tied to his toe. And even if he wanted to go down and take one last look, paying a grim call of respect, he couldn't. Even if he wanted to have a part in that grotesque, morbid protraction of unavailing sorrow called a funeral, he couldn't.

And of Julie Steadman he knew nothing. Except that she was buried. Julie! He wondered now what kind of a life he might have had with her if things had gone the other way. And safe from conscience, wondered if behind the dam that was his love for Gordy, there wasn't always a more violent river of wanting her than he ever dared admit. In any case, a useless and unworthy speculation.

Memories of them, isolated, disjointed but full of the motion of living personalities in changing attitudes, flicked past in the vividness of total recall. But, like the images of a failing projector, the pictures slowed, stopped altogether, began again: Julie on a night ribbon of lonely road, in a splash of rushing light, her hands thrown up,

38

palms out in that feeble gesture to protection from two
tons of hurtling metal—ramming, gouging, flinging the rag
doll high, to fall broken on the ground.

And Gordy in the dark of the house. Oblivious in
sleep. Or staring in a chair, lost in his own pictures. And
the hand with the gun reaching out of the darkness to
sight close to the temple, squeezing the trigger, the little
finger of lead with mindless obedience, poking out his
life.

Oh, the brutal treachery, the waste, the loss. Corwin
was filled with monumental words, maudlin and smother-
ingly oppressive. He shut it all off. Relief in action, that
was the only way. Play the part. Play it gay and buoyant
and careless, hiding behind the mask to the end. Play it
coolly unthinking. Play it to win.

He left the drink unfinished and mounted the stairs.
The little "Office of the Manager" sign, with the hand
pointing, was on the brink of a hallway which was off the
lounge. He followed it to an open doorway.

At sight of him, a man stood behind the desk in the
small room.

"You Mr. Milano?"

"That's right, sir."

"I'm Corwin. Todd Corwin."

"Sure, sure, come in. I told Floyd Whitlock we'd fix
you up. Glad to do it."

Milano had the sort of naturally dark skin which sun
turned almost chocolate. He had a narrow build, dark
hair and precise features, emphasized by the austere trim
of a small mustache. He wore gray slacks, an open white
shirt rolled to the elbows. He was losing ground on forty,
was operating-room clean and handsome in the same impersonal degree of shining surgical instruments.

His cool scrubbed hands lifted a pack of cigarettes.
"Smoke?"

"No, thanks."

"Well, sit down a minute."

They sat.

"Whitlock says you'll be here a few days to look over
the Bennett Anchorage."

"At least a few days."

"That would be a good buy for someone—Bennett's. Andy Bennett takes good care of his place. Neat, very neat. In good repair all the time."

"Oh?"

"Of course, Andy is touching seventy and wants out. His son, Dolf, has no interest—plays with hot-house flowers. Horticulture, isn't it? Yes, well, flowers and boats, you know—never the twain—" Milano chuckled dryly, tapped a cigarette incessantly on a manicured thumb. "Have you made an appraisal out there yet?"

"I'm practically fresh off the plane."

"I see. Well, tell you what. I could fix you up with a locker and you could act like a member while you're in town. Then if you decide to take over Bennett's and remain, I'm sure we could have you voted in officially. Meantime, I could lend you anything you need. Play tennis, swim?"

"Both. And I have all the gear. Sure grateful to you, Mr. Milano."

"Everyone calls me Charlie. And don't mention it. Whitlock is an old friend and a damn good cop. Just because they—well, anyway, come on with me and I'll find you that locker."

He followed Milano down a path to the men's bathhouse, dressing room or whatever they called it. A sort of oversized hut with benches and rows of lockers, a john and showers, all of it having the slightly damp, vaguely acrid smell of all such places where men gathered to wash away the sweat of exertion. Milano showed him a locker, found the appropriate key and they went outside.

"Courts are just back there," he pointed. "Half a dozen, busy all the time. Swimming pool there and if you can't find the ocean, holler for a seeing eye. No real golf, but there's a little putting green right below by that cluster of trees."

"I'm strictly tennis, anyway," said Corwin.

"Good. Let's go see if we can find you a game."

Before he could object, Milano was moving off to the courts. He wondered if Milano noticed that he wasn't even dressed for it.

They hiked around the courts, most of them in use. Two women played together haphazardly, not nearly as well as the ten-year-olds stroking beautifully on the next court. There was a game of doubles—four men, two of them heavy at the belly and ponderous on their feet. Then a weathered, thin man who must be sixty playing a marvelously constructed brunette in her twenties. Their performance seemed flawless.

"Usually," said Milano, "you'll find one or two sitting out on the sidelines and we can get up a doubles or another singles. No luck today. Maybe if you wait around."

"Sure," said Corwin, "I have to change anyway. I'll bet one of those kids or the old guy there could trim me, as much as I've played lately."

"Those kids belong to Mr. Goetz of Buckner and Goetz, a law firm. They'll be playing tournament tennis one day. The old guy, as you call him, is the pro around here. Harry Lockridge." Milano's smile had an edge to it.

"Sorry. He looks pro, all right."

"And he is old." The edge came off Milano's smile. "But he's the best in town when it comes to lessons."

"Is that right? The girl doesn't look like she needs lessons."

Milano's smile disappeared altogether. Nothing replaced it. The expression was merely blank. "She doesn't take lessons any more," he said. "There are some people you can't teach. She just buys playing time from Harry and calls it a lesson."

"Who wins?"

"They take turns. Harry lets her beat him once in a while. Good politics."

"Interesting. Who is she?"

Milano's eyes flicked up and settled on him carefully. Corwin could almost hear him ticking.

"That's Gail Vollmer," he said. "Well, shout if you need anything."

He turned and went off briskly, his feet lifting and falling in precise rhythm.

Chapter 4

Todd Corwin opened the gate and stepped onto the court where Gail Vollmer and the pro were playing. He was dressed in his tennis clothes now, carrying his racket. He sat down on a bench at mid-court and watched. They were unaware of him.

She would flip the ball high into the air and come smashing down on it with such power that it arrowed over the net cleanly, bouncing safely and whizzing off from a corner placement. Her return was fast—hard, with a long graceful arching. She played like a man, while every line of her denied masculinity.

Her cool black hair fell straight to the shoulders where it turned up neatly. The bangs were straight also and the effect was total simplicity. Forehead and cheekbones were high, face oval, chin a little haughty. The mouth dipped and swelled at the lower lip, the upper wide and straight. The eyes had a suggestion of Orientalism, color indeterminate at the distance.

The legs were long, the waist slender, buttocks high, small and firm. In those moments when she stood on tiptoe poised for the serve, her breasts were long-thrusting and conical beneath her blouse.

About her there was an air of dominance, a hint of quick temper and smoldering resentments.

Corwin decided he wouldn't like her, even less because he was irked to find that she stirred some animal response in him. It would be difficult to form an objective opinion. She was a Vollmer. The hell with it. She was a means to an end.

Sooner or later, as he expected, a ball bounced off the back fence and came his way. She was moving after it and he delayed, missing it on purpose, retrieving it as she approached.

He dropped the ball into her hand, looking into her

eyes. Gray-green, he thought. Like the ocean in the threat of storm.

"You'd never make a ball boy, would you?" The smile was borderline between sarcasm and tease.

"Sorry," he said. "So terribly out of practice. Please give me just one more chance. Please?"

Her brows went up, her eyes discovered him, head to toe. She went off.

The next time, the ball came within a few feet of him, rolled beyond. He sat comfortably, unmoving. When she came near, he pointed. "I think your ball went that way, Miss Vollmer."

"*Touché*," she said, picking it up. "And who are you?"

"Why? Would it change anything?"

"I doubt it."

"I'm crushed."

"I can tell that. I can't remember seeing you around. I don't think I know you."

"No? That's funny. They all know me down at the Y. Weren't you at the dance?"

"What dance?"

"At the Y."

"Don't be an idiot." Her eyes flashed.

"You're holding up the game. Your partner's waiting."

"He's on my time. You play?"

"Not since Wimbledon."

She smiled, this time without rancor. "I could take you six-love," she said.

"You might take six, but I don't know about the love."

"You want to try?"

"Love?"

"Tennis!"

"I might."

"After this set then." She pranced off with a fine show of rump.

She beat Lockridge in two more games. He didn't seem to be trying. He departed with a wave and a look of secret amusement.

She took the first set six-three, while he warmed up. From there on his serve carried the viciousness of his feelings, his return was vengeance directed. It seemed a grudge game, even on her part. They spoke little. He won the next two sets 6-4, 6-4.

Her brow was damp, but still she looked cool. Surprisingly, she said, "That was good, very good. Thanks for the licking."

"Do you always thank the winner?" he said, smiling. The game had given him a small release. He felt better.

"That's the trouble," she said. "I seldom have anyone to thank. I love to be beaten. Otherwise, there's no challenge the next time."

She tucked the racket under her arm and walked off the court. He fell in beside her.

"Really, what's your name?" she said.

He told her.

"You're not local, are you?"

"No. Here on business."

"How did you know me then?" She stopped momentarily, looked at him, then moved on.

"Doesn't everyone?"

"In town. Not in the whole world."

He was silent.

"Swim?"

"Okay. Ocean or pool?"

"Pools are tame," she said. "I'll meet you on the beach in about . . . ten?"

"All right."

They separated.

He found her lying on the beach in a yellow Bikini. The lower half hugged her body like a diaper. The upper was not much more than a cap for the high peaks of her breasts. In between, the flat brown tummy. All that was visible, and that was most of her, was richly tanned.

He was irritated because he couldn't take his eyes off her. He didn't want to think of sex. Didn't want to be distracted from his agony, his purpose.

"Now do a little dance," he said.

Unconscious of her body, she looked up at him, shading her eyes. "What took you so long?"

"I had more to put on," he answered.

Her eyes climbed from blue trunks to bare chest and joined his. Her lips pursed. "France is that way," she said, pointing. "Race you to Le Havre. Come on!"

44

LAMENT FOR JULIE

She catapulted off the beach and hurled herself into the water, diving cleanly through the first wave, continuing in stroke without loss of motion. She was just a white bathing cap and a windmill of brown arms in the distance before the water was over his head.

He took his time, feeling sullen, remote, not up to the task of violent play. She swam back to him, salty beads of water standing on her cheeks as they treaded water.

"At your rate, we'll never make the boat train to Paris by nightfall," she said, punctuating her words with little gasps. Her face was reproving, as if her intent had all along been serious.

"Busy, busy, going nowhere," he said. My God, but she had energy. She didn't taste life, she consumed it. "What are you escaping—thought?" The guilty dare not rest. Oh, Christ, would he ever have a normal reaction?

"Listen," she said, "does my charming personality clash with yours or are you one of the angry men I've been reading about?"

"You mean you take time out to read?"

"That does it," she said, and pushing water in his face with the heel of her hand, made strenuously for shore.

He caught her by the shoulder as she was running up the beach.

"I'm sorry," he said. He wasn't, but he had been on the verge of defeating himself. Control, control.

"Are you?"

"Yes."

She fell into a heap on the beach, he beside her. "Well, I really don't mind." She smiled.

"No?"

"No, because in an odd sort of way you're refreshing."

"Why?"

"My life is full of grinning yes-men."

"I see."

"No, you don't. Tell me, what would a type like you earn his living at?"

"I own boats in Florida. Cruise ships for the sightseers."

She nodded. "Yes, you have rather nautical eyes."

"Far-seeing?"

"Salty. Stinging. And why are you here?"

45

"Last question?"

"For a while."

"I'm going to look over Bennett's Anchorage. I might buy, I might not. Now tell me about the Vollmers. I know nothing but what I hear."

"What do you hear?"

"Money and power. The Vollmers speak and there can be only one answer."

"Not the Vollmers—Austin Vollmer, my father. He does the speaking. We're just satellites."

"Yes, but even a satellite has power by association."

She came up on one elbow and peered at him sharply. "Everything you say sounds so personal. But you're interesting." She fell back again, a hand over her eyes.

He watched the slow rise and fall of her breasts and wanted to twist something steel-hard until it broke.

"This is one of the few places I ever drink before dark," she said. "It always seems like night in here."

They were in the club bar below the waterline of the pool. She wore a mint-green sun dress, her hair was brushed shiny, she had added a touch of lipstick. She was drinking Scotch on the rocks.

"Don't apologize," he said. "If you want to drink, drink. Have another. Make it four."

She was gazing at one of the portholes behind which fish swam lazily. Her eyes were unfocused. He knew she merely stared, saw something interior which gave her face the same absent look of one who is doing sums in the head or reaching for a name on the tip of the mind.

Her eyes snapped to his suddenly. "What's that? What did you say?"

"I said, have another. Make it four."

"Did you ever feel like getting tight for no particular reason?" she asked.

"No. There's almost always a reason if you look for it."

"But then," she continued, "you should never get tight with strangers."

"Is that one of your rules?"

"You've got to have rules. Otherwise, you can't have the fun of breaking them."

He ordered two more drinks.

LAMENT FOR JULIE

"You play good tennis and you swim well," he said. "I suppose you dance and go to the usual parties and night spots of your set. What else do you do?"

She laughed, a brittled sound. "Is there anything else?"

"Work, a purpose, some ambition."

"You sound idealistic, Todd. So you'll be disappointed. I have no reason to work and I have no ambition to change the world. If I have a purpose, I guess it's pleasure —until I find a better one."

"At least, you're honest about it."

"I can afford to be honest."

"It's a luxury, all right," he said.

"Everyone judges you by their own standards, Todd. If *they* have to work, *you* should work. But suppose you had everything you could possibly need. Would you go right on with what you're doing?"

"I don't know. Not if I could keep from being bored."

"That's a sore subject. I'm bored most of the time. It's one of the penalties." She held up her glass. "Let's drink to relief." Her glass came back to the table empty.

He ordered another. She gulped half, said, "I'm not bored now. Not in the least. You're a challenge, Todd. I'd like to unravel you and take a look at that dark brooding thing in the center. But I'm feeling these drinks too much. Let's go for a ride."

"Where?"

"Well—we have a beach house. Would you like to see it?"

"Sure. Why not?"

In the parking lot she moved directly to the Lincoln. She opened the door, turned. "I forgot to ask. Do you have a car?"

"I had to rent one. Buick over there."

"Why don't we pick it up later and go in mine."

"Okay."

She drove skillfully, but very fast, gunning ahead of traffic, swerving back into line just in time, crowding the curves.

"Are you tight, or do you always drive this way?" he asked mildly.

"Always." She flashed a smile. "I like the pace. Everything, everyone, has to have pace."

47

LAMENT FOR JULIE

He was going to say something about the police, then remembered she was a Vollmer. Her attention became fixed on the narrow two-lane skirting the shore. A pedestrian, a girl carrying schoolbooks, walked toward them, head down, unmindful. In the seconds before she flipped by, she became Julie Steadman, mouth open in horror, arms upraised. He wondered if those long-fingered clever hands held the wheel on that night.

They came to a village, slowed, halted for a stoplight. A kid moved among the cars with papers. He bought one. The Longport *Daily News*. International politics, a Chicago train wreck, a holdup monopolized the front page. He turned to the second.

It was there under a small caption: DESPONDENT WIDOWER A SUICIDE. One paragraph. It said that Gordon Steadman, apparently grieving over the loss of his wife in a hit-run accident, shot himself during the night. A neighbor discovered the body when she saw the front door standing partly open in the early morning and went to investigate. Steadman had just returned from sea duty in the submarine service. Relatives were being sought. That was about it. The story was a masterpiece of understatement.

He saw that she was watching him covertly as the village slid by and they returned to speed. "How do you like our paper?" she said.

"What do you want me to say? It's a paper. I don't know much about the newspaper game. At least they don't bomb you with a lot of local junk. Mostly national stuff here."

She chuckled. "Typical out-of-town point of view. When you get national datelines from the wire services, that just means there's nothing doing here. And that's most of the time."

"Oh, I don't know," he mused. "Here's a story about some local yokel who shot himself. Came home from sea duty and went out of his head because his wife was killed in a hit-run. Strange. Lots of pathos there, too. Yet your paper gives it just a few lines." He kept his face disinterested but watched her intently. "Could have gone front page with that one."

She never took her eyes from the road, but she was too

48

long in answering. "Well," she said, "we don't play up the sensational. It's a conservative paper. On the other hand, maybe they didn't have time to get in all the details. The story might break big tomorrow."

"Maybe," he said. "That's probably it. But I'll tell you this. If I was married and I came home and found my wife was a hit-run victim, I'd catch the bastard and kill 'im before I'd knock myself off."

She didn't answer. She hardly spoke the rest of the way. She only drove faster.

Chapter 5

They swung onto a gravel road posted A. L. VOLLMER. NO TRESPASSING. The road wound through a sandy wasteland of dunes, wild grass and trees. It passed a cove with a sturdy dock and a wide green boathouse. It sliced through a vine-matted wall of yellow brick and came upon a spit of land—a neat spread of flowered grounds, the ocean, a house. The house sat on a high framework above a garage, was long and straight, had much glass and wood and Oriental flavor—the new Japanese look. It fronted on the ocean. In the background to the right lay a heart-shaped swimming pool.

"This is it," said Gail Vollmer.

"Spectacular," Corwin murmured.

"Officially, it isn't open yet."

"What do you do—have a ceremony?"

She pulled up before the garage. "I mean, we don't live here full-time except in August. We come down on week-ends and occasionally for a swim. I love it. Even in winter —moody and bleak and wild."

They got out and he followed her around front to a curve of stairway that reached above to a door. As they climbed, the long brown spindles of her legs preceded, the high tight weave of her buttocks filling his vision. Ocean sound was lifted on a briny wind, the torpid peace of late afternoon sun touched his face. The liquor was still warm in his belly, he felt the lazy elbow of desire and his mind was, for once, blank.

"The height is mostly for view," she explained, opening her purse. "But once in a while there's a storm, or the tide is too high. Then it's practical."

"Mmmmm."

She found the keys and they went in.

There was a long sweep of living room. A great fireplace dominated one side of the room. A white carpet of deep pile spread itself beneath the long, low curve of a sectional sofa, enormous chairs, an immense driftwood coffee table, a semicircle of ebony bar. Lamps in twisting irregular shapes mushroomed everywhere. White, gold and black flamed with red, formed the color pattern.

"I like it," he said, watching her adjust a window, cross to the bar.

She opened an inset refrigerator and there was the sound of ice in a bowl. "Every room faces the ocean. That's why the house is so long. Let's see . . . Scotch, rum, burbon. More bourbon?"

"Please. On the rocks."

He wandered about, pausing at windows, staring down at the fan of beach, the green and white dapple of ocean. The rich in their cloistered world of beauty and plenty. Did they ever pause to think what they had? Did they ever compare their holdings with those shoddy ones of the poor? Were they ever grateful? For, if you had neither gratitude nor awareness, you had nothing. You moved amidst selfish abundance but it was never yours. For fleeting moments it belonged, rather, to those like himself who came and really saw.

She set the drinks with their coasters on the driftwood table. They settled upon the sofa and drank in silence. He watched her obliquely. The fun, the spirit or whatever it was, had gone from her face. She leaned forward and tapped a cigarette incessantly. The soft skin was drawn tight, a corner of her mouth twitched.

"For God's sake, don't just sit there, Todd. Say something!"

LAMENT FOR JULIE

He turned a steady gaze upon her. Again he felt volatile.

"Why are you so nervous?" he said. "The world is your great big fun-house. Why are you so nervous then?"

"I don't know, I don't know. But sometimes you—"

"I what?"

"Make me nervous. Frightened. You seem so intense and at the same time—I really don't know. Aren't you enjoying yourself? Please be gay."

"Gay, gay," he said.

"Let's do something."

"Like what?"

"Anything. Another swim? Or we could take the speedboat. A Century. It's very fast. Oh, I don't care, anything." She stood.

"Anything," he said. "Just anything. Just keep moving, right?"

"Oh, goddamn, goddamn," she muttered, twisting her hands together. "You make everything sound like an—an accusation."

"At the rate you're going," he said calmly, "you could get hysterical."

A hectic smile flickered across her face, caught and held. She stopped twisting her hands. "That's right, I am being silly. Too many late nights, too many hangovers. Little things become exaggerated."

She sank back beside him, closer than before, her head resting on the back of the sofa, eyes watching him. "I'm sorry," she said. "You're so contained, I envy you. What could disturb you?"

Her mouth was a moist insinuation. "What could disturb you?" she asked again.

"Your mouth." The words came obediently, with the suggestion that he could now wreck his gains or take command of his purpose. He kissed her and against his will he thawed immediately, became mindless. Her arms came around him, her tongue searched and probed, draining memory of names like Gordy and Julie and . . . Vollmer.

His hand cupped the long heaving swell of her breast and he was surprised that he could have made himself oblivious to so much woman for even an interval. And if he had a weakness, she had found it.

Briefly, they separated. "Oh, lord, lord," she whimpered, "now I know what it was I really wanted to do."

He sought the zipper at the back of her dress. It came down with a small metallic sigh. He spread the dress away from the brown-gold of her shoulders, kissed them. "Oh, lord, lord," she repeated. He found the bra snaps and, as he fingered them apart, she pulled down the dress.

Sun touched the soft bronze molding of her breasts at the wide beginning of their thrust, followed the narrowing and lifting to the end of tan, touched the sweet cone of white, the pink-brown of nipples. Again he kissed the hollow of her shoulder and let his mouth drift down, down. "Heaven, heaven," she moaned between clenched teeth, and pulled his head close against her.

But suddenly she had wrenched away. She was up and covering herself. She slipped across the room and looked out a window to the road. She tried the door, bolted it, came back.

She looked down the hall and, following her gaze, he stood. They embraced. They walked together until they came to a bedroom. Inside she closed the door. She stood uncertainly in the center of the room.

"Would you believe me if I told you it's been a long time since anything like this has happened? Only once before, when I thought I was in love."

"It doesn't matter," he answered. "But I understand the need to say it."

He waited.

"What will you think of me—later?"

"I don't know," he said, meaning something else entirely and, at the same time, wishing women didn't always, always have to justify and rationalize their way into bed.

"Oh, I don't care, I don't care," she said.

Swiftly, she began to undress.

For a moment he watched her with ambivalence, pushed toward her by a giant hand of desire. And all against his will, beyond desire, driven to her by an unphysical needing which he had not known since he had been caught in the first flush of love for Julie. Yet wrenched from even the thought of such treacherous unity with a Vollmer.

But when she stood naked, the fragile underclothes heaped at her feet, watching him now with an expression close to awe, her smile at once piquant and tender, he went to her in a kind of trance and gathered her in his arms. While he kissed her with a harsh pressure of his lips that was next to anger, while his hands caressed her back, followed the neat contour of waist downward to the firm-soft rise of buttocks, her eager fingers opened the buttons of his shirt, fumbled at the buckle of his belt. Until he made a sound in his throat and frantically finished what she had begun.

The big bed was pliant beneath them, the sheets were cool and had the silk-smooth feel of luxury. They lay side by side wrapped together. She pressed against him, gentle fingers kneading his shoulders.

He felt urgent, demanding. But she said, "Don't hurry, darling. I'm a hungry animal, but I'm a woman, too. Say nice things to me, be kind."

"Kind, kind, kind," he said through clenched teeth. "I don't know the meaning of that word. I've forgotten. What would you know about kindness?"

"Oh, everything. Everything! And I'd show you. If you'd only let me. If I could only reach you in that hard place where you live."

He didn't answer, couldn't answer. Had to protect the core of himself. Instead, he made a quick shift of position. And looking down into glazed eyes and open lips, probed her body with a fierce thrusting, as if he wanted to give and take pleasure, yet inflict pain.

And after a time, she made a sobbing sound, and gave a long sigh. Then she said, "Why do you hate me, Todd? Oh, why do you make love to me as if you hate me!"

Really, it was perfect timing. For they had just then come out of the bedroom and she had fixed a drink and they were talking in the strained sort of way which follows first intimacy, when they heard the car. Tires crunching gravel.

They looked at each other and together they crossed to the window.

The woman or girl, for she was quite young, was driving. The chauffeur, in uniform, also young and good-looking in an oily-dark sneering sort of way, sat next to her on the passenger side. In unison they alighted. Then, seeing the Lincoln, which had been out of view at the far side of the house, the young woman motioned the chauffeur back. There was something furtive in his look and the manner in which he returned so quickly to the car.

The car itself was a black-top convertible Cadillac with a blazing red finish, polished to a mirror glaze. Corwin could not see the plate and did not have to. He knew he was looking upon the instrument of Julie Steadman's death. And knowing, the shiny automobile gathered identity, took aura from the fact, became somber and deadly as a weapon still bloody from the kill.

"Who's the girl?" he asked.

"You'll meet her soon enough," said Gail. "I hear her little feet on the stairs." Her jaw was canted oddly, her tone was sharpened with malice.

She didn't go to the door but let it be opened with much key jangling and lock turning.

The young woman was a redhead—perhaps artificially, but if so, with expensive artifice. The hair was long, lustrous and caught in a flowing pony tail. The young woman was slight, with a wiry tension about her. Coming across the room, she seemed to move on springs. Her little jewel of a face had sharp, clever eyes, the pouty mouth wore an expression of glee, off-beat, slightly malevolent.

She carried a riding crop, was dressed in jodhpurs and a white blouse, under which her narrow saucy breasts stirred with her movements. She seemed not more than a year or two older than Gail, though a look of shrewdness worked against the impression of youth.

"Ahhh," she said, "Gail, dear. I didn't know you had company. In fact I didn't know you were here until a moment ago."

The tone was saccharine, dissolving in acid.

"Joy, this is Mr. Corwin. Todd Corwin."

"You forgot the last name, dear. I'm a Vollmer, too, Mr. Corwin."

54

.

"Is that so?" said Corwin. "I didn't know Gail had a sister."

"Oh, but I'm not her sister." Her smile was like a knife slicing the words. "I'm her mother."

"Need I add the obvious?" came back Gail. "My step-mother."

"I was on the way back from the riding stables," said Joy, ignoring the remark, "and I thought I'd check the supplies. I'm thinking of a beach party over the week-end."

"Why didn't you let Tony come up and help you? He's so handy, don't you think?"

"I'll just have a look," said Joy Vollmer, bouncing off with a side glance at Corwin and then disappearing down the hall.

"Would you excuse me a minute or two, Todd?" Gail said.

"Sure. Take your time. I'll go below and wander around."

She smiled and departed.

He went down the stairs and sauntered over to the pool. The water appeared to be purest blue. He knew it was only reflection from the bottom surface. Hands in pockets, he moved leisurely in the general direction of the red Cadillac, strolling, glancing about, apparently killing time.

He came abreast of the car. The chauffeur, cap pushed back on his head, watched from behind the wheel with unfriendly eyes. Corwin passed in front of the convertible. Suddenly he came to a halt, bent down, inspected a tire, straightened.

"Looks like you need air in this one," he called to the chauffeur referred to by Gail as Tony. He knew the tire was of a type which showed a slight bulge, even at normal pressure.

Tony got out of the car with a pained, disbelieving expression. He had broad shoulders, a lot of chest, below which his body tapered swiftly to narrow waist and long legs. As he approached, Corwin stepped back, crouched, pretending to eye the tire from the inside front, but actually giving close inspection to the paint on the right front fender, matching it against the hood. He had to stare, close his eyes, stare again before he caught it. Both surfaces had the same gloss, but the fender had more color tone, a brighter, richer red. There was also a tiny teardrop of red paint on the glass of the headlamp. He could find no scratch or dent.

Meanwhile, Tony was bent over the tire. As Corwin joined him, he straightened, gave the tire a kick, shook his head. "Nothin' wrong with it," he said. "Plenty of air. Plenty. You must drive a small car. These big tires, they're low pressure. Always look like they're squashed down. Nope, she's okay."

Tony had a long loop of a face, heavy lips and bushy brows over small black eyes. His skin was swarthy and minutely pocked around the chin. His dark hair needed cutting in back—he grew sideburns. He had the sullen, arrogant look attributed to the motorcycle and hot-rod fraternity, though post-graduate, for he must have been in his mid-twenties.

"Well," said Corwin, "I guess you're right. That bulge had me fooled."

"I keep my cars in good shape," said Tony possessively. "Tires and all."

"Sure looks nice," said Corwin. "Like a big red mirror. Sweet job."

"Yeah," said Tony, taking off his cap, wiping sweat from his brow.

"Fast, too, I'll bet."

"Not so fast. Big musclebound motor—power but no top speed. You don't get that off an assembly line."

"You ever take her out on some country road and open her up?"

Tony replaced the cap, adjusted it, eyed him with cool black insolence. "No place you can do that around here. Say—who're you?"

"I'm Miss Vollmer's guest. And who are you?"

Tony's face closed, opened again with the beginning of awareness. He offered a twist of smile and glanced down at his uniform.

"That's right," said Corwin. "And don't forget it."

He walked off.

Mrs. Joy Vollmer was coming down the stairs and they met halfway.

LAMENT FOR JULIE

"Have a good time now, Mr. Corwin," she said with a hint of second meaning. "Or may I call you Todd?"

"Certainly."

Smiling, she leaned back against the rail in an attitude which pulled the jodhpurs tight around her abdomen, pushed the cones of her breasts towards him. "It's good to see a new face around," she said. "Very pleasant. Perhaps you'll come to our little party this week-end."

"Perhaps."

"I'll be expecting you then, Todd." She touched the riding crop to his shoulder where it caressed a moment like an extension of her hand before she fluffed down the stairs, her pony tail bouncing behind.

He stood with Gail at the window as they drove off in the red Cadillac, backing around so that now he could see the plate with its V-3 license. Tony was driving, Joy Vollmer now upright and proper in back.

"It's a beautiful color," said Corwin. "Kind of a blood red." Blood on blood, he thought.

She turned her head quickly but he didn't meet her eyes, didn't have to. He smoked and watched.

"It's much too gaudy for my taste," said Gail. "But it's her favorite."

"Is that right?" The car was amost out of sight, a red blotch receding. "I have an idea your tastes differ a great deal. In other ways, I mean." He looked at her now.

She frowned, bit the tip of her tongue. "We have only one mutuality—men. She has a peculiar habit of liking exactly the same men I do. Plus one or two loathsome characters of her own choosing."

"My, my. What does your father say?"

"My father is very busy. And much older. He bought her like he would some flashy diamond—a stickpin he wears on special occasions. Of what she does when she's not sparkling for him, he knows nothing, sees nothing and hears nothing. Who would dare tell him?"

"You're not jealous of her, are you?"

"The other way 'round. I just hate her. She's an amoral bitch! Oh, come on. Let's get out of here."

Chapter 6

Night had come. They had returned to the club to pick up his car. Gail had wanted to stop for a drink and they had gone to the bar. They sat at a table. One drink became two.

"You must be hungry," Gail said.

"So-so."

"Too late for dinner at my house. It would have been dull anyway. But there's always something. We could scrounge around."

"Don't you have a date tonight?"

"I did. But I broke it. I called up when I went to the little girl's room a few minutes ago. Was that presumptuous of me?"

"Yes. But I don't mind."

"You don't have any plans?"

"Not until tomorrow."

"Bennett's?"

"Mostly. That's what I came for."

"You're staying at the Plaza, didn't you say?"

"Right."

"I think it's silly."

"Silly?"

"To stay at a hotel when there are so many Vollmer bedrooms perfectly empty."

"Oh, now listen, you hardly know me."

She gazed at him steadily. The corners of her mouth twitched. "You exaggerate, darling."

"See what you mean."

"Really, Todd, this is a rare thing with me. I don't know how to explain it."

"It's not necessary to explain. Or to have a conscience. About some things."

"Will you stay with us?"

"No. But thanks anyway. There would be certain obligations I couldn't meet—the little formalities. I have work

58

to do and I have to come and go a great deal without bowing in and out."

"Why don't you stay at the beach house then? No one would bother you. Of course, it would be lonely . . ."

He considered. He hadn't wanted to stay at the Vollmers' city home because while he could watch them, they could also watch him. But at the beach house he could hold the contact and still have freedom. The whole thing was fantastic, invited to the enemy camp, so to speak. The ways of the rich. If contained hatred made you appear hard to get, they were intrigued and you could borrow a slice of their world.

"Okay," he said. "The beach house. You're very hospitable."

She opened her purse and gave him the key. "Just pick up your things and go on out there tonight whenever you're ready."

"Thanks. But be sure to tell the powers that be. I don't want to get shot as an intruder."

"Don't worry. I'll fix it up. It's not unusual. Lots of friends of mine stay there from time to time. There's plenty of food but all the servants are up at the other house, so you'll have to—can you cook?"

"Sure. But I'll just get my own breakfast and eat out the rest of the time."

"You can use the uh . . . the same bedroom."

"Oh, fondly."

She smiled. A secret little smile. How much evil knowledge lay behind those Vollmer smiles? He would find out. Yes, he would find out. For Gordy. And Julie. Oh, God! Oh, Christ! Did it really happen?

"Tell me," he said, "what is it like to be very rich?" He couldn't quite imagine. Twenty thousand net was a very good year for him. "What is it like to have everything, absolutely everything you could ever want, Gail?"

The question seemed to surprise her. She frowned. She looked away and back again. "What is it like? Why, I don't know. I never think about it. It has no meaning for me. It's nothing."

"Oh, come on now. Everything is nothing? That's no answer."

"All right. If I must. I know it sounds awful, but the

59

truth is, you get used to it. Nice things surround me everywhere. I hardly notice them any more. If I want a dress, fur coat, a trip to Europe, spending money, I simply ask and Dad gives it to me. But I already have everything and I didn't work for it and it's meaningless."

"Can't you make it mean something by comparing yourself with the poor?"

"Not really. Only in an academic sense. For example. You live in Florida and in the winter you know that while the sun is shining and it's eighty and you're at the beach in your bathing suit, around most of the rest of the country people are freezing. The skies are gray, there are no flowers, the trees are bare and the landscape bleak. But does that mean anything to you, really?"

"No."

"You see? I have so much but I'm too close to it all and it's nice but not exciting."

"You must have some needs, some problems."

"I do, Todd. I do. They're all intangible, emotional. My father gives me things. And I want what he doesn't know how to give—love. Joy—I hate to call her my stepmother—she . . . well, she's another problem. Oh, lord, there are always problems, there's always trouble. Trouble, trouble, trouble."

"That's what you've got right now, isn't it? Trouble. Something's eating you. That's how we got together. I'm a distraction for whatever it is that's gnawing away inside you. Right?"

"No! That's unfair."

"I'm a good listener, Gail." He leaned forward. "Want to tell me about it?"

"No," she said. "You wouldn't understand. You couldn't possibly. No one in the whole world could possibly understand." She pushed her drink away. "Do you mind if we go now? Please. I can't sit here another minute."

"Run, run, run," he answered. "See how they run."

Chapter 7

They were in the den of the Vollmer house in a quiet
suburb of Longport. He supposed they didn't even call it
a den, but a library. It was a big square room with a
high ceiling, dark paneling, an ocean of books contained
by wall shelves on either side of the fireplace. There was
a vast Oriental rug, leather chairs, a great desk, the in-
evitable bar and a glass-enclosed case of guns, expensive
rifles for the hunt. A rather formal place without warmth,
but still a retreat. For it was dwarfed by the living room.
    The house itself was an enormous old colonial type,
full of classic but gloomy antiques. It sat in showcase
spendor on the brow of a hill, down which a lawn of golf-
course dimensions rolled between a full-dress parade of
majestic trees, green-decked guardians of the royal palace.
    There was a tennis court, a pool, a four-car garage,
servant's quarters above.
    A colored girl in a black uniform with a serrated white
apron had brought them a buffet of turkey, ham and roast
beef with appropriate trimmings upon Gail's mention of
the need for "a bite to eat." The remainder, enough to
feed twelve, had barely been removed, when they had
visitors.
    Both young men were tall and in their new twenties.
Both wore sport coats and slacks, white shirts and ties.
Though their physical appearance differed markedly, there
was about them the suggestion of imitation. Or at least
conformity, as if both enjoyed the same fraternity on the
same campus.
    The dark-haired one had a crew cut over triangular
features, terminating in a sharp scoop of jaw. He had a
wide mouth, a short thin nose and deep circles under the
eyes. His look was both cocky and focused, as if everything which came under his glance was a subject for
minutely critical and disdainful attention.
    The other had long sandy hair, combed straight back

over a high forehead. His face was a neat oval of pale skin and delicately handsome features, almost effeminate. In a faintly smug but pleasant sort of way, the face was apparently pleased with itself, sophisticated, at ease, ready to smile and charm.

The young man was slim, with long arms and long-fingered expressive hands.

"We interrupting anything strategic, sis?" said the dark-haired one with the focused look.

"Yes, you are, Matt," said Gail, straight-faced.

"You mustn't leave," said Matt, showing his palm briefly before crossing to the bar, followed by the other. "Warren and I are just going to have one for the road."

"What road tonight?" said Gail.

"The same. Soft women and hard liquor. What else?"

"Matt, old boy," said the one called Warren. "We forget our manners. A stranger is in our midst." He walked toward Todd with his loose casual gait, smiling, smiling, his boyish charm turned on.

Reluctantly, Corwin rose for the farce.

"My name is Warren Grimm. And you, sir?"

"Todd Corwin." He took the soft-looking, hard-squeezing hand.

"Warren is a reporter, junior grade," said Gail. "At the *News,* of course. Almost the only one in our bright circle who does anything at all. Very ambitious."

" 'Junior' is a measure of service, not ability, Mr. Corwin. But Gail is not feeling magnanimous."

"And over there, oblivious at his true calling behind the bar, is my little brother Matt," said Gail.

"Hi," said Matt, without looking up from his task, but waving a hand behind the bar.

"Drink, Gail?" asked Warren Grimm.

"Not now, thanks."

"Mr. Corwin?"

"Thanks, anyway. Too full of food."

Warren took the drink Matt offered him and both fell into chairs, Warren sitting almost straight, a little bent forward, alert, interested, Matt with one leg draped over the arm, his expression suggesting a rather nauseous smell in the air.

A face that will always look a little hostile, thought

Corwin. Immediately he found himself wondering if that was the face behind the windshield of the red Cadillac. How long, how long before he would be able to think and act without suspicion and hate?

"What brings you to our town, Mr. Corwin?" Warren Grimm asked pleasantly.

"Brings?" said Corwin, irritated by the remark because Grimm already knew he wasn't local. "What makes you think I'm a stranger? Or do you know everyone in a town of over a hundred thousand?"

"Oh, no. Not by far. But you have a certain look of importance," said Grimm sagely. "And I know all the important people."

"You've done wonders for my ego."

Grimm raised his glass in a small salute and drank.

"Going to be with us long, Corwin?" asked Matt Vollmer.

Corwin wondered if he could possibly be referring to the length of his stay as a Vollmer guest. No, where would he have come by that information? "I'll be here a few days or a few weeks, I don't know," he answered. "It depends on Andy Bennett. I'm trying to buy his anchorage at my own price."

"Well," said young Vollmer, "you couldn't go far wrong if you decide to take over Bennett's. Most everyone has some kind of rig rusting over there. Let me know if you have trouble with the old sonofabitch. He's got the first and last penny he ever stole. But I might get the Old Man to loosen him up a bit for you."

"Obliged," said Corwin.

"One more for the dusty road, Warren?"

"For the road, Matt."

They swallowed with much clinking of ice and took their glasses to the bar.

Corwin and Gail looked at each other.

"Well," said Corwin quietly, "they seem to know all about me."

"In this house," answered Gail in the same undertone, "everyone knows almost everything about those who enter these lusty halls. It's a form of self-protection. But you're one of the few persons I know who has nothing to hide. Aren't you?"

63

"Comparatively, I'm as open as the public library."

"I must catch up on my reading." She chuckled and was silent.

Warren Grimm moved listlessly about the room with a drink in his hand, paused at the rack of guns behind the glass case, opened the door and fingered a stock idly.

"Hands off the Vollmer arsenal," said Matt, approaching.

Warren ignored him, set down his glass and plucked a shining beauty from the case. He examined it casually.

"Good gun for you," said Matt dryly. "It's for elephants. Put it back, it might be loaded."

Warren continued to hold the gun, smiling with lifted eyebrows and a look of tolerance. "Don't be a jerk. Of course it isn't loaded."

Matt took the rifle away from him, sighted around the room until the barrel made a half-circle and came to the exact center of Warren Grimm's chest.

"You said it's not loaded, Warren. Okay if I pull the trigger?"

"Shoot if you must, this young blond head," said Warren still smiling.

"Chest, chest," said Vollmer, "I can see the young blond hairs on your chest." He lowered the gun, cocked it. "Look," he said. "You picked this gun at random, right?"

"Right."

"It could have been any gun in the case, right?"

"Right."

"So I'll make you a sporting proposition. I don't know if the gun is loaded. Why should it be? And you don't know. So give me two to one odds. I'll bet you fifty to your hundred it's loaded."

"Bet!" said Warren, reaching in his pocket, searching through a roll of bills, dropping several on a table, while young Vollmer placed a single bill of his own on top.

"Okay," said Grimm. "Open 'er up and let's see."

"Not that way," said Matt, raising the rifle again to chest level. "The odds are all in your favor so you've got to have guts."

Grimm sides-stepped neatly, saying, "No bet," and picked up his money.

LAMENT FOR JULIE

"Chicken," said Vollmer. "Any other takers? Gail? No? How about you, Corwin?" He raised the gun until Corwin was looking across the room directly into the round evil eye of the barrel. "Put up your hundred, Corwin. One little squeeze and you've got yourself a sucker's jackpot."

Corwin sat very still. He knew it was a stupid gag and yet a whisper of intuition compounded by his secret knowledge gored his stomach and bristled the back of his neck.

"Put down that goddamn gun, Vollmer," he said, spacing each word.

Vollmer held the gun steady, sighting, drawing a slow breath.

"Matt!" cried Gail.

Corwin remained still. "I'm not going to tell you again," he said. "Drop that gun!"

Grimm reached out suddenly and shoved the barrel down. "For chrissake," he said. "Why don't you grow up!"

"Oh, for crap sake, I was only kidding," said Vollmer. "What a bunch of cotton spines. The gun was never loaded. Look, I'll show you."

He brought the rifle to his shoulder quickly, aimed into a corner of the room and pulled the trigger.

The gun jerked, the room was heavy with exploding sound and the smell of cordite.

Matt Vollmer's mouth fell open with an expression of amazement that was well acted or very real. "I'll be goddamned," he said. "I'll be goddamned. I would have won the bet." He began to laugh, richly at first, trailing off to giggling, an odd sound, almost hysterical.

Corwin took the rifle out of his limp hands, placed it back in the case, returned to stand face to face with Vollmer. In his mind, in his muscles and fists, he could already feel the sweet release of all that was pent up inside him battering against flesh, bone, teeth of that giggling face.

Grimm stepped between them. "I know how you feel, Mr. Corwin," he said. "But don't do it. He's just dumb enough to think that was funny. And he's not worth it. You hit him and you might as well hit his Old Man, Austin Lamar. And I'd rather hit the mayor or the sheriff. They'd be better enemies. See what I mean?"

"No," said Corwin.

"C'mon, Matt," said Grimm, "before the man takes you apart. I might even help him, so c'mon." He half led, half shoved Vollmer out the door.

His fingers working, Corwin followed, watched until they were gone.

"Oh, I wish—I just wish you had hit him," said Gail. "Of all the vacuum-headed, dangerous stunts."

The colored maid came into the room with wide eyes and anxious expression. "What happen, Miss Gail? Sound to me like a shot. You all right?"

"I'm all right, Betsy. Just another little noise in a madhouse. Now run along and forget it."

The maid gave her head a little shake, saying, "Oh, my," and departed.

Corwin found the bullet hole in the baseboard, ran his finger over it, crossed the room and fell into a chair beside Gail.

"I wonder," he said. "Is the kid crazy, or very, very smart?"

"A little of both." She hadn't caught his meaning. "Todd, I'm terribly sorry. I don't know what to say."

When he didn't answer, she went on in a gush of words. "It's lucky Warren Grimm was here. He's got sense. He's so mature, I wonder why he bothers with Matt. I have a feeling Dad asked him to look out for Matt, and he's proud of that. You might say the Grimms are the second family in this town. Does that sound smug? Well, it is true. Mr. Grimm owns the Plaza where you're staying, a big lumber company, I don't know how much real estate and he's board chairman of the leading bank. They're very wealthy. Warren just fools around at the newspaper for kicks. His father could fix him up almost anywhere. Are you listening? Please say something."

"I have nothing against Grimm," he said. "A little in love with himself, but altogether a pretty decent sort."

"Yes, well, I hope you're not entirely disgusted with us. Matt is spoiled and selfish and brainless, sometimes, but I don't think he's vicious. I'll tell you this about him, he—"

She looked up and he followed her gaze. Three men had come into the room so quietly, he hadn't heard. The tall one with the lean long-jawed face wore the uniform of a sheriff. The shorter of the other two, the bellied man with the cigar, detached himself and approached.

"Dad! Do you have to sneak in with the whole police force?"

"Out, Gail," he said quietly. "Take it somewhere else. I'm going to be busy in here."

So this was Austin Vollmer. If he noticed Corwin, there was nothing to indicate it. He had a soggy mouth, heavy chin, a Roman nose and impatient eyes of pale glacial blue. He wore expensive clothes in careless disarray, as if reluctant to make this one foolish concession to social mores.

"With the amount of traffic in here tonight," said Gail, "you would think this was the one room in the house."

"That's right," said Austin Vollmer. "The one room in the house and I want it. Now get your fanny out of here."

"Dad, this is Todd Corwin. We met at the club. He came here from Florida to buy Bennett's if he can come to terms. I told him he could stay at the beach house awhile."

"You did, eh?" Vollmer's eyes slid sideways. "I'll run into you then, Corwin. We'll talk. I know all about Bennett." He sniffed the air. "What's that stink in here, Gail?"

"Your cigar, Dad."

Corwin had been standing, but Vollmer strode off without offering his hand.

As Gail closed the door, Vollmer was already behind the desk, the sheriff was seated and the other was drawing up a chair.

"I think I'll shove off," said Corwin as they crossed the vast living room.

"Don't go. Dad isn't always so rude. He has things on his mind."

"I imagine." He continued on to the door.

"That was Sheriff and Wade Utterback, a detective chief. They seemed all business or I would have introduced you."

"Does your father have a lot of business with the police?"

"Not much. It's probably something political. Sheriff

67

is an elective office and Gifford needs some backing for re-election in a couple of months."

"I see. Strictly political then." Corwin opened the door. "I thought maybe it had something to do with that accident."

"What accident?" The words leaped from her throat.

"Let's see now—I heard the name and I've forgotten. But it's right on the tip of my . . . Got it! Steadman. Mrs. Steadman. Wasn't that the name of the woman who was run down!"

Her face was perfectly blank. And yet he could sense behind her eyes the stealthy metamorphosis of her thinking.

"Steadman?" she said after what seemed an interminable silence. "Oh, yes, that dreadful hit-run thing. I did hear about that. But what's it got to do with us?"

"Why, I don't know. Just a rumor I heard at the club."

She swallowed. "What rumor? What did you hear?"

"Nothing, really. Something about one of the Vollmer cars being involved and then it all got hushed up."

"Don't believe everything you hear, Todd."

"Oh, I don't. Just curious. It's amazing. If you're up there on top of the pile, everyone wants to bat you down. Anything to destroy you. The fear of money. The fear of power. I suppose that's all there is to it—fear and jealousy. But naturally I wondered how such a filthy rumor could get started unless there was some truth in it."

There was a silence.

They stared at each other.

Unblinkingly.

On and on.

Chapter 8

He awoke with an unfamiliar sound gaining on his ears—
a rushing, liquid whisper. The uncaught tail of some
tense and somber dream sent him rolling out of bed,
stumbing across the room to the window.

Sunlight spread itself beyond the shadow of the house,
over the white-gold of the beach, the blue-green of the
ocean foaming the shore. And he knew he was at the beach
house, guest of an evil man called Vollmer.

He had slept long. The sleep of escape from loathsome memories. It was nearly ten. He rubbed his eyes,
went into the adjoining bathroom with the ebony basin
and the white tile and the sunken ebony tub. A little
jewel of a room. Expensive. With a clean scrubbed smell.

He brushed his teeth, shaved and showered. Dressed, he
went to the kitchen, found oranges, made toast and
coffee. He ate without desire, in defense of hunger. He
felt alone and once more exceedingly depressed. He had
the feel of an angry mechanism, set in motion against
impossible odds. He was without will to stop until he was
dead, though the victory would be unsweetened by anything more than a useless revenge.

And he would be dead. It came to him surely, with the
image of a round black eye widening in the barrel of
that high-powered rifle, staring him down. A twisted
joke? Or a means to another accident ("My god, I didn't
know it was loaded!"), with his body tagged in the
morgue, filed away next to Gordy Steadman until some
relative guaranteed payment of burial.

He was big and physically powerful. And mentally
sharp—sensitive, aware of danger. And yet he knew if
they meant to kill you, sooner or later they would do it
and nothing could stop it.

He moved about the living room with cup and saucer
in his hand, sipping. He couldn't sit still. Not even to
think.

LAMENT FOR JULIE

He came to rest before the great panel of glass, looking down again upon the beach, the ocean. He thought, how beautiful and how empty. Unshared. Then, far to the left, his eye caught change and delayed. Something on the beach. No, not something, someone. Supine and so motionless, so like the surrounding sands as to be almost in camouflage.

It was a woman. She was perfectly naked. On her back, with head resting on folded arms. Her mocha tan was unblemished by pale skin anywhere. Even to the topmost swell of her breasts, she was all of the same perfectly even color.

It wasn't Gail. His memory of her size and contour was still clear in his mind. It was someone else. He had already guessed when he went downstairs and out the door.

He stood atop a dune and looked down upon her just below. Joy Vollmer was facing the other way, her red pony tail stretched out across the sand, her eyes closed. Her arms were extended, hands flat and palms down, fingers spread, as if to catch sun in every pore and crevice of her body. The toenails of her little feet were painted a burgundy color, matching her fingernails. A few feet behind her lay a pale-pink, terry-cloth beach robe, all in a heap, as if shrugged from her body in one careless gesture to freedom. He could see no bathing suit or other clothing.

Her body was like her face, a perfect little jewel of hard clear lines, all unblemished. Yet, he was disturbed by the sight of her in only the most abstract way, for he was too full of trouble. And, anyway, total nakedness, without the subtle preparations for it, was more startling than exciting.

He wasn't sure what to do. Ignore her? Or make his presence known in some oblique manner. He decided to ignore her and was about to leave when her eyes flew open, she sat up and turned towards him.

"Well, my God," she said, her face unshocked. "Why didn't you knock?" With that she flung over on her belly, exposing a neat arch of tan buttocks, her long narrow breasts pressed into the sand with the soft bulge of them all that remained in view.

LAMENT FOR JULIE

She stretched her hand and tried to reach the robe, but it was an impossible distance.

"Please," she said, "be a good gallant knight and fetch it for me. I'm not about to play Godiva without a horse."

He came down the side of the dune without a word and, picking up the robe, draped it over her. Then he moved off a yard or so while she fumbled.

She came to his side, tightening the belt. "I thought I was completely alone," she said. He knew she was lying, even though his car was in the garage with the door closed. "I come down here two or three times a week in the summer for the sun treatment and there's hardly ever anyone about until August."

"Sorry," he said.

"Oh, that's all right." She began to move toward the house, squinting up at him as they kicked through the sand. "I don't blush easily, not any more."

"Didn't Gail tell you she had put me up here for a few days?"

"Well, no. I haven't seen her. But you're certainly welcome, Mr. Corwin. 'Mister' doesn't sound right after the unveiling. Is Todd okay?"

"Fine." They had been through that routine before.

"You're not very talkative, are you?"

"Words are only a fence."

"A fence? Around what?"

"Around the truth."

"Ahhh. He doth not speak, but thinketh much. I like that. Have you had breakfast?"

"Thanks. I found something."

"Don't take such big strides. I'm only a little girl."

"Are you?"

Her warm little hand sought his and grasped, so that he pulled her along.

"Listen, why don't we go for a swim?"

"Left my trunks at the club. Nothing to wear."

"Are you ashamed?"

"Yes. Besides, I have things to do. It's a business trip, primarily."

"Well, why don't you unbend and have a little secondary fun?" She gave a lilting intimacy to the word fun. They had climbed the stairs and he opened the door.

"Fun is for the very rich," he said. He closed the door behind him.

"Not all fun is expensive. Besides, I'm buying." She moved dancingly toward the bar. "Drink?"

"At ten o'clock?"

"The sun won't tell."

"All right. Bourbon and soda then." He didn't want the drink but sooner or later all the Vollmers had to be probed in depth. He might not get a better chance.

He crossed the room with purpose and looked down upon the gravel drive. She had brought the red Cadillac. Metal assembled at a factory with machines and impersonal hands. Yet, he hated it. Loathed the sight of it. Hated it!

"You drove it yourself," he said, the words sounding, even to himself, harsh and accusatory. "Where's the chauffeur?"

"Tony? He drove Mr. Vollmer."

"Do you always refer to him as 'Mister Vollmer'?" Why couldn't he control the bite in everything he said?

She looked at him curiously, all but head and shoulders lost behind the bar.

"I call him Mr. Vollmer because I think of him as Mr. Vollmer," she said with a tight mouth.

"I find that revealing." He turned again to a grim contemplation of the red convertible.

"Oh, you should, you should." Her voice approached behind him, accompanied by the tinkle of ice.

He took the glass from her hand and sipped thoughtfully. The pink robe was loose at the shoulders, and where the cloth crossed to make a V, her breasts nudged each other and like golden missiles, went thrusting away out of sight.

"That's a really handsome automobile if you like the color. Your personal car?"

"There are no personal cars, no personal anythings. Mr. Vollmer owns it all and merely lends." Her tone nailed him up and left him crucified.

"All right, so you borrow that one the most." His smile tried to remove the sound of inquisition.

"Yes, because I like things that glitter. I know it's

childish, but there was a time when everything around me was drab and old."

"I think that car is fascinating," he said. "In a gruesome soft of way."

"Gruesome?" She looked quickly down to the car and back to him. "Why gruesome?"

"Because there's a rumor trickling around town that a red Cadillac convertible belonging to the Vollmers was in a hit-run accident."

"An accident? What accident?" Her face struggled for composure.

"A girl by the name of Steadman, I understand. Julie Steadman. She was killed, wasn't she?"

"Steadman?" Joy made a frowning, contemplative face. "Oh, yes. I remember reading about it in the paper. But heavens, it wasn't our car!"

"It wasn't?"

"No. Certainly, if it was, I would have been the first to hear about it."

"Especially if you were driving the car yourself."

"Now, wait just a minute, Todd. I don't know who you've been listening to, but it so happens that on that particular night I didn't have the convertible. In fact, I didn't go out at all."

"How can you be sure? How is it that you remember so well?"

"Really, now. You sound so, so accusatory."

"I'm only curious."

She was silent. Then she said, "Well, I do remember clearly because there was a discussion about it at breakfast the next morning. And Gail was so odd. She refused to let us talk about it, said it made her sick. And, well, I hate to say this, but she's been acting strangely ever since. As if some awful thing was on her mind."

"Now, who's accusing?" he said sharply.

"I'm not accusing at all, just stating a fact. Besides, it may have nothing at all to do with the accident."

"Sure, sure. Then who did drive the car that night? Was it Gail?"

"I can't say. All I know is that she planned to use the convertible and probably she did. But I didn't see her

73

go out and I didn't see her come in. Anyway, you admit the whole business about the convertible is just a rumor. So let's drop it."

He didn't want to drop it. But one more question and Joy would know he had a personal interest. Damn! Goddamn! Was it Gail? Was it! Whom could you believe?

"Okay," he said. "Let's drop it. Let's hear about your Mister Vollmer. How did you meet him?"

"Oh, that's a beautiful, beautiful story. I was a cashier in the restaurant of a hotel where Mr. Vollmer used to stay in Washington. He was at this hotel for something like a month soon after his first wife died. And he would come up to the counter and pay his check and buy a cigar and grunt at me, giving me what he thought was the sexy eye. And then the grunts got to be words and one night, just at closing, he offered me a thousand dollars to go upstairs to bed with him."

"Just like that?"

"Just like that."

"And why do you tell me all this?"

She took a long swallow and he watched the pulse of her throat. "Because I can only talk to strangers, people who are never a part of the town but just come and go. That's why I tell you." She cocked her head and looked up at him with amusement. She was enjoying herself. "And because I'd like to shake you loose from your moorings, Mr. Todd Corwin. Either you're a stuffy bastard or you smolder inside the way I do—and we're alike. Now, do you want the rest of it?"

"I wouldn't miss it."

"All right. So he offered me a thousand dollars," she said into her glass. "Have you ever seen my husband?"

"I've seen him."

"Then you can guess what was passing through my mind. I saw that sloppy mouth around the soggy cigar and the fishy obscene eyes and the pot belly. And I thought, *This guy would have to offer a thousand and you'd earn it.* But he didn't look like a hundred, let alone a thousand, so I told him to go to hell.

"He opened his wallet and counted out ten one hundreds, watching me. I kept my face like stone, but I was amazed and the sight of that money was making him look years younger. It took off twenty pounds. Because I was earning forty-five a week, living in a coal-bin bug trap of a room and giving myself to a junior clerk for a few beers and a movie on Saturday night. In that money I saw three rooms, nice and clean and cutely furnished in a neighborhood where a girl could walk home at night without looking back over her shoulders, and new clothes and maybe even the down payment for a little second-hand car.

"Well, he pushed the pile of hundreds toward me and he said, 'Take it and put it away. I'll trust you. Be knocking on the door of room six-two-one in an hour. If you change your mind, put the money in an envelope and send it up with a bellhop. But do one or the other. And take my advice. Don't try to skip. I'd find you and I'd fix you good.' Then he just walked off, as if he had bought me and it was just a matter of delivery.

"I looked at the money and I counted it and I looked at it again. Then I stuffed it in my purse. I was off in about twenty minutes and I went to the lobby and paced up and down, thinking, thinking. Finally, I told myself, *What the hell, this one time, with my eyes closed and my mind walled off from knowing or caring, like a zombie.* So I went up there and knocked on the door and he wasn't in the least surprised. I was with him twice more that week and I almost got used to it.

"Then, he made me a proposition. If I would marry him he would put a hundred thousand in my name at the bank just before the ceremony. And then I could go live with him in the mansion in Longport and have the servants and the clothes and the cars and the rest.

"I hated him but I had no love for anyone else either, so I decided I would take his filthy money and after a while I would just disappear with it, get a divorce. But he was smarter than I was. He let me run wild, spending my own hundred thousand on this, that and everything that came before my eyes, insinuating there would be more. But there wasn't. And I had spent it all. And I was trapped. Because I liked the way I was living and I couldn't ever go back to any other way. And he had made up a pedigree for me and given me importance in the town.

75

"So I stayed on, borrowing his houses and his cars and his servants and his big name, but having nothing of my own. Of course, I really won in the end." She laughed harshly. "Because now I lock my door at night. He's my husband, but he can't get by begging on his knees what certain others can have for a smile. If you only knew what certain others. The irony of it. The irony, the irony . . ."

Her laughter broke around her in little convulsive waves that sounded more like sobbing. It was almost as if he should put his arm around her to comfort her. But the day would never come when he would comfort a Vollmer.

"What is it between you and Gail?" he asked. "Why do you hate each other?"

She stopped laughing. "Maybe I wouldn't hate Gail if she didn't hate me. But that's impossible. She loved her mother and I'm too young and too cheap in her eyes to ever be a substitute. I'm just her father's permanent call girl. And when you're treated like a call girl, you come to act like one. There are things which have happened—Never mind. When I'm hurt, I just fight back, that's all. Another drink, Todd?"

"Thanks. But I have to go."

"Stay awhile and we'll talk." She drew closer, rested her head on his shoulder. "I'm awfully lonely, you see. For my kind."

He knew that he could have her and he knew why. She was an outcast, a Vollmer in name only. She had never been accepted. Gail was of Vollmer blood, entrenched, secure. And Joy had to keep proving that she could take what belonged to Gail, even such a temporary holding as he appeared to be.

Corwin moved away from her, set his glass on the bar. "There'll be other times," he said. "I'll be around. We'll have a long talk. Yours is a fascinating story. I want to hear all of it."

"Are you really interested?" she said, running a hand over his lapel.

"Oh, very," he answered. "You have no idea."

"Then why don't you show it? Why don't you go swimming with me?"

"That's a different kind of interest," he said, smiling wryly. "Besides, I thought we went over that swimming bit before."

"Yes, and you said you didn't have time for play. And here you are sitting around chatting with me as if you had all the time in the world."

He couldn't think of an answer for that one. How could he explain that for him this was no idle conversation?

"Anyway," she continued, "a good guest does something to please the hostess *once* in a while. And, darling, in a sense, you are *my* guest, too."

"I repeat, no trunks. I left them at the club."

"Really, Todd. Now, really! You don't look like a shy man to me."

Well, he thought. *She's an insistent bitch. And if she resents me she'll make trouble. Better to keep harmony— on the surface.*

"Okay," he said. "Just a dip. You go and get ready."

"Ready?" She stood suddenly and let the robe fall to the floor. "Darling, I'm ready! What about you?"

He had forgotten that she was naked beneath the robe. She stood with her shoulders back so that her narrow pushy breasts were thrust toward him. He tried to stare at her objectively and was irritated because he couldn't quite make it. The pulse of desire was eternally without conscience.

"Yes," he said, "I guess you're ready, all right. Aren't you always?"

Her face tightened, her eyes were bright stones of anger. But only for an instant.

"I'll ignore that," she said. "For the time being. Especially since dignity in the nude is difficult to manage." She smiled impudently.

"Well, at least get a goddamn towel or something," he snapped. Standing, he began to peel off his clothes. "You'll find me in the water. Look hard, it's a big pool."

Still smiling, she draped the robe about her shoulders and went off to another room.

He was about a hundred feet offshore when he saw her coming. The sea was placid to the horizon. Cool and lucid, a pastel green with tints of blue. He had been swimming parallel to the coast with deep powerful strokes,

77

venting the turmoil that seemed always with him. He slid cleanly through the water, loving the slick feel of it on bare skin. He paused, dove to explore the bottom, came up, and spied her. Carrying towels and a beach robe, she raced naked across the sand, breasts heaving, the white-gold of her body glistening in the sun.

She dropped robe and towels to the sand and without losing stride, broke into the surf, swam toward him. Breathless, she came to rest two feet from him, treading water.

"Don't you love it, Todd? Don't you love it? I mean, the feel of it. Nothing stops you, no itchy suit to hold you back."

"Mmmmm."

In the clear sea he watched her legs piston, followed the firm outline of her body. It seemed magnified to lusty proportions, shimmering, radiant.

"Are you always so passive, Todd? Doesn't *anything* excite you?"

"A good fast game of croquet gives me goose flesh."

"I'll bet, you mallet-head." She snickered, came close. Their bodies touched. "Did you ever make love in the water?"

"Not in the water. Under the water. Where I come from we call it skin diving. Is that what you mean? Love at ten fathoms? Great! You should try it."

"Oh, I will, I will." She pushed closer and her breasts touched his chest. Her hand roamed under the surface, caressing him, teasing.

Suddenly he grabbed her and kissed her. She entwined her legs about him and, forgetful, they sank slowly in a salty embrace. He paddled upward. Gasping for air, they broke apart. Laughing, she palmed water at him. "Race you for shore!" she cried.

She splashed off without waiting. He watched her a moment, undecided. Then he followed, easily overtaking her. They scampered out and fell upon the beach robe.

"Dry me," she said.

"Certainly, your highness."

"Please?"

He picked up one of the towels and rubbed it briskly across her back.

"Not so rough, darling. That's it. Now the front?"

He made a lazy swipe at her shoulders, moved down to her breasts.

"Aw, the hell with it!" he growled, and tossed the towel aside. "How much can you take?"

"How much can you give, darling?"

"Okay, that's it! You're gonna find out!"

He pushed her down and sank with her. Nails clawed his back and he hardly knew it. Her mouth twisted under his, teeth clamped his lip.

"My God," he moaned. "Why do they let you out of the cage?"

"Oh, I'm a cat," she hissed. "Wild, wild. Tame me, tame me!"

And he did. And for a time she lay back with sleepy, half-lidded eyes, an expression of smug satisfaction on her face. And all at once he felt debased. Knowing that he had been used. Knowing that he was just another of Joy's conquests, the act a whip with which she lashed at Vollmer, the fire of her body kindled for his destruction in effigy.

"I have to go," he said, trying to hide his disgust, his self-loathing. "I have some business to take of."

"Business, business. But you'll be back, darling, won't you? Now that you've learned the difference between a woman and a child."

"What does that mean?" But he knew exactly, of course. If he would transfer to Joy the interest he was supposed to have in Gail, the vengeance would be complete. For a time, Joy's jealousy would be appeased.

"It means nothing, really," she said. "Will I see you tomorrow? We could take another little swim and go on from there."

"Sure," he said. "See you tomorrow."

He stood, pretending that he did not notice the hand which lazily beckoned him to a parting kiss. Now ashamed of his nakedness, he quickly fastened a towel around his waist and strode off.

He looked back once. Her face was blissful, complacent. Eyes closed, she lay supine, a golden offering to the sun.

Chapter 9

He made a point of going first to Bennett's Anchorage. He had to maintain the pretense or become suspect. He found the old man in a little office off the showroom with its display of boats and boat supplies.

Bennett was a dried-out, bony little man with a great mass of disordered, perfectly white hair. He had sun-parched, freckled skin and watery eyes. He spoke so softly as to be almost inaudible and there was in his manner a suggestion of the ascetic. He seemed incapable of driving anything like a hard bargain—an impression that was quickly erased the first minute his price came under discussion.

Meanwhile, Bennett took him on a painstaking inspection of the slips and docking facilities, the grounds, the dry storage yard, the work sheds, the equipment and boats, new and used. Corwin was able to ask a great many educated questions, for there was nothing shown him he did not understand. He had a thorough knowledge of boats and everything pertaining to them.

Back in the office, Corwin spent some time going over the books, said if he was interested he would have an accountant check them and give him a detailed report. He then pretended to haggle over price, justifying his position with intelligent observations. Bennett was adamant, even raising his whisper of a voice and looking almost angry. Corwin made certain that they were never separated by anything less than thirty thousand, though hinting that he was still pliable.

They parted in friendly disagreement, Corwin promising to come again after he had given it more thought.

From a pay phone, Corwin called Floyd Whitlock, the ex-detective who had been fired from the Longport homicide squad. Corwin explained his progress with the Vollmers and Whitlock seemed pleased. For once his tone was not quite so negative.

LAMENT FOR JULIE

Whitlock said he had begun a sneaky investigation of his own, that he was slowly warming a cold trail to the whereabouts of the Lansky couple. He would admit no details on the phone, but he did say that he had gone out twice in his car and both times he had been tailed by a man unknown to him, or at least unrecognizable in the dark. Himself an old hand at tailing, he had lost the guy after some adroit maneuvering.

Whitlock agreed that, at the moment, there was little chance of finding out who murdered Gordy Steadman and the best approach was by way of Julie Steadman. The who and why of Julie's end was the key to both deaths and hers was the trail to follow.

Whitlock said finally that he did not want Corwin to think the Longport Police Department was hopelessly corrupt. There were highly placed factions under the control of Vollmer politics and Vollmer money. There were also the honest but frightened elements who could only work with absolute evidence. Whitlock felt that if he could bring in that absolute evidence, even a Vollmer would be brought to trial and he, Whitlock, would be restored to his job. And, further, there would be the newspaper support of the much smaller, but not unheard voice of the Longport *Evening Bulletin*.

"Don't forget," said Whitlock in signing off, "there's only one thing deader than evidence against a Vollmer— and that could be the guy looking for it. Play it cozy, son. And keep in touch."

However unlikely the possibility at this juncture, Corwin began to watch his rear-view mirror for a tail, when, after talking to Whitlock, he steered for the house in which Julie had lived and Gordy had died. No one followed, but he parked two blocks away and walked.

He told the thin blotchy-faced woman who answered at the house next door that Mrs. Steadman's life had been insured, the benefits would now go to her mother and he was investigating the circumstances of her death. Especially since there was a double indemnity clause for accident.

The woman, whose name was Mrs. Keeler, seemed flattered to be the subject of attention.

"If the poor girl was run over," she said, logically,

81

"why I just can't see any need to prove it was an accident."

"You're perfectly right, Mrs. Keeler," he said. "It does seem a little absurd. But our company has certain regulations for every type of case. And in a hit-and-run, when there are no witnesses to the circumstances of death, we must make a routine investigation. It's merely a matter of company policy." He took a notebook from his pocket and readied his pen.

"I see. Well, of course, I didn't know the Steadman girl. I mean, not as a friend. I would meet her coming or going and we would chat for a minute or two, pass the time of day. Nothing more than that. She was a pretty little thing. My, yes. Stunning! No wonder her husband couldn't live without her, poor man. I met him, too, you know."

Mrs. Keeler had her hair up in curlers and her face was a naked island of white skin upon which angry volcanoes of acne erupted. Her lips were thin and dry, her dark eyes feverish with the need of acknowledgment. Her hands were busy, touching her hair, her throat, a button of her dress.

"Now," said Corwin. "Do you remember the night of the accident?"

"Oh, yes, looking back, quite well."

"Did Mrs. Steadman have any visitors?"

"No, no, I don't believe so. This time of year our windows are always open and I would hear a car. Then, of course, we're so close I would see anyone who came to her door. I never spy, heaven knows. But you can't help seeing what's right in front of you."

"Of course not. Then she went off alone?"

"Yes, on foot. She had a car but she didn't drive it. I don't know why unless she didn't want to bother with parking in town. Easier to take the bus up at the corner."

"She was going to town?"

"To the movies, I think. She mentioned it earlier."

"Did she ever have any visitors?"

"No, not that I remember. Not anyone who ever went inside, that is." Her smile said she understood the direction he was taking and enjoyed it. "But once someone brought her to the house in a car. A man."

"Did you know the man?"

"No, I never saw him before but——"

"Did you get a look at him?"

"That's what I was trying to say. I didn't really see him. She just hopped out and he sped right off."

"What kind of car was it?"

"Oh, heavens, I don't know one from the other."

"Color? Was it red?"

"No, maybe gray or beige, something like that. A rather small car. It seems to me there was something printed on the door, but I'm not sure."

"Something printed on the door," he repeated, and wrote in his notebook. "Tell me this, Mrs. Keller, in your conversations with Mrs. Steadman, however brief, did she tell you anything of interest about herself?"

Mrs. Keeler shook her head firmly. "She hardly ever talked about herself. Just general things."

"Did she seem happy?"

"So-so, I guess. Like everyone. Oh, now wait a minute! She did mention one personal thing, sort of offhand. She said her husband was getting out of the navy and when he got home she was going to have a job to surprise him. I gathered they could use the extra money."

"Did she mention what kind of job?"

"She said something about taking want ads for the newspaper. She was going to see if there was an opening."

He wrote hastily in his book. "And when was this?"

"Let me see—not—not more than a couple of days or so before she was killed, I think."

"Well, thank you very much, Mrs. Keeler. I think that's all for now." He closed the book and dropped it in his pocket. "If there's anything else, we'll contact you."

"Yes, be sure and let me know if I can help. Poor people, I'm always glad to——"

"Thank you, and now if you'll forgive me, I have to run. Good-bye."

He hurried off before she thought to ask his name and company.

He was only a few blocks from the offices of the Longport *Daily News* when he saw the police car coming up behind him. The cruiser was not moving swiftly. It simply drew up and lay behind. Probably it was a routine patrol of a main thoroughfare, but he couldn't fight the tension which made him grip the steering wheel and grow rigid in his seat.

He checked his speedometer. Thirty in a twenty-five-mile-an-hour zone. Maybe that was it. He slowed. In a moment the patrol car came abreast. Two uniformed officers. The one on the passenger side turned his head slightly in passing and gave him a cool impersonal glance. Or was it impersonal?

Damn! A little thing like a traffic patrol and he was in a sweat.

The car turned a corner ahead and disappeared. He relaxed.

The want-ad section was just to the right of the main lobby. A long counter behind which a couple of girls sat on stools, working with customers. Beyond them, in the background, more girls typing. He asked for the head of the department and a plump gray-haired lady with an in-charge-and-no-monkey-business face approached, asked what he wanted.

"I'm with Southern States Mutual Life," he said. "Need a little information about one of our policyholders."

"Yes, sir. What's it got to do with us?"

He took out his notebook, flipped pages. "The young lady may have been employed here. Let's see . . . name is Steadman—Julie Steadman, 1423 Peacock Drive."

There was nothing in the woman's face. She merely tightened her jaw. "Steadman? I'll check it. Just have a seat, please."

It seemed to take a long time. Too long. He had wanted to duck out quickly. He fidgited.

He was looking out into the lobby, but actually his sight was inward. He was only half aware that someone going past the alcove was turning to stare at him. And then he saw that it Matt Vollmer.

Young Vollmer's lips moved but he said nothing. He turned away quickly and strode into an elevator.

The chances were a hundred to one against such a thing happening. And yet it had happened—the police car had happened along and the gun had happened to be loaded. All accidents?

The woman with the in-charge face signaled him and he returned to the counter.

LAMENT FOR JULIE

"I have the information for you," she said. "Mrs. Steadman applied for a position in this department but the vacancy we had advertised was filled. She was referred to the personnel office upstairs. I called and they told me Mrs. Steadman had been hired for secretarial work but that she never reported for the position. That's all we have on her, sir."

"Thank you," he said. "I won't need anything else."

He made notes, waiting until she had gone into an adjoining room. Then he slipped a ring off his finger and put it in his pocket. It was a gold ring, not very valuable. One of the girls was free and he gave her an ad for a lost man's ring, a diamond with a gold mounting bearing his initials. He offered a reward and asked for the replies to be sent to the paper's box number. He paid for the ad and got a receipt.

As he was tucking the receipt in his wallet, a haughty-faced chesty blonde came up to him, breathless, purposeful.

"Are you Mr. Corwin?"

"Yes."

"Mr. Vollmer would like to see you, sir."

"Which Mr. Vollmer?"

"There's only one Mr. Vollmer, sir," she said fatuously. "I'll show you to his office."

He followed her to the elevator and they rose to the third floor. They passed the length of a great room of many desks, row on row. Shirt-sleeved reporters and other personnel bent themselves over typewriters. From somewhere came the intermittent voice-garble and static of a short-wave radio monitoring police calls.

At the far end of the room they climbed a short flight of steps. They were in a narrow hall. Beyond a door marked RADIO NEWS BOOTH was another, marked A. L. VOLLMER, PRESIDENT. They entered.

The reception room contained leather chairs and a sofa, two desks. A girl typed at one, the other was vacant and probably belonged to the blonde. She crossed the room, knocked on a door and opened it in the same movement. She stepped back to let him pass and closed the door behind him.

It was a large corner room with windows overlooking

85

LAMENT FOR JULIE

Broadway and a narrow side street. Across an expanse of maroon carpet behind an enormous square of desk, sat Austin Vollmer in a swivel chair. An American flag poled upward obliquely from a corner. An immense portrait of Vollmer in oil dominated one wall and looked down upon him approvingly.

There were some group photographs, meaningless to Corwin. The rest of the room contained the usual array of leather for seating. Basically the office was plain, austere.

Vollmer was swiveled away toward the window, showing his back. He talked into the telephone softly. Cigar smoke made a jagged ascent above his chair.

Corwin was damned if he was going to stand there like the office boy and so he approached. Just then Vollmer grunted something, swung around, dropped the receiver in place and looked up.

"Come in, come in," he said, chewing the words with the cigar. "Have a seat, Corwin."

He took a chair and waited. Vollmer puffed a moment, removed the cigar and studied it.

"My son said he saw you in the building and so I thought we might have a chat."

"I lost a ring," said Corwin. "Quite valuable. I came over to place an ad."

"You did the right thing," said Vollmer. "Big circulation. We'll find it for you. Comfortable over at the beach? Anything you need?"

"Not a thing, Mr. Vollmer." He was damned if he was going to play the grateful act.

Vollmer stuck the cigar in his mouth, clasped hands behind his neck, leaned back and swayed. Right, left, right, left and return, smoke trailing.

"Came to our humble city to buy the Bennett place, did you, Corwin?" chewed Vollmer.

"Providing I can get it at my price, of course."

The cigar came out. "Seems to me you could find better deals in Florida. Plan to settle here permanently?"

"Oh, no. I think not. I'll put someone in charge and fly up now and then."

Vollmer nodded. Pudgy hands behind head, the swing began again. It was a nowhere conversation. It waited to reach the area of Vollmer's real interest.

LAMENT FOR JULIE

"Well, since my daughter has made you a Vollmer guest, I'd like to help you on the Bennett deal, Corwin. I'd like to see you wrap it up."

Now it was coming, he could sense it.

"What is Bennett asking for his outfit? Give you a price, did he?"

"He came down from a hundred seventy-five to a hundred seventy thousand. I'm offering a hundred forty."

Vollmer chuckled, coughed, chuckled again. "A hundred and forty. I'd like to have seen Bennett's face. If he was thirty years younger and had another hundred pounds, I'll bet he'd have tossed you out on your ass. You're a remarkable fellow, Corwin. A real trader. Why that anchorage would be a steal at a hundred and seventy grand." He aimed his cigar. "And you know it."

Corwin's fingertips gouged leather. He wanted to flatten the smug murdering bastard, choke the truth out of him.

"Look, Vollmer," he said. "Unless you're acting as go-between, I'd prefer to decide for myself how much Bennett's place is worth to me. Your business is newspapers, mine is boats. I know what I'm doing."

Vollmer smiled. "I like you, Corwin. You've got guts. Staying at my house, traveling with my daughter and then sassing her old man."

"I could be out of the house in an hour," said Corwin.

"You see?" said Vollmer, still smiling. "What did I tell you? Guts. Independent. Fearless. Now don't get sore, Corwin. I was just goosing you a little. I like to see what's inside a man before I do him any favors."

"I'm suspicious of favors," said Corwin.

"And you're right," snapped Vollmer. "Always be suspicious. I'm a very suspicious guy myself. And it's paid off. Yes sir, it's paid off for me. And I have an idea it'll go right on paying. Because, you see, Corwin, in a small burg like this if you don't watch yourself, someone else will be watching you. See what I mean?"

"I don't need glasses."

Vollmer hacked, rolled back and stood up. He crossed to the window, stood with his hands folded behind his back, puffing. "You really want the Bennett place?" he said over his shoulder.

87

"That's what I came for."

"I see. That's what you came for. You're sure, now?"
Corwin didn't answer. Couldn't trust himself.

Vollmer came back, sat on a corner of the desk, leaned forward. "Tell you what, Corwin. I'm a man who can make things happen around here if I want to. I can shake people loose you couldn't move with dynamite. I can pick up that phone and make this town dance to my tune—a hundred thousand hotfoots, all jumping at once." He took off his glasses, rubbed his eyes.

Corwin watched him coolly, raging inside.

"I can do things with Bennett, too, Corwin. Because I know where he's tender. I know where he lives. I make it my business to know about everyone." The glasses went back in place, enlarging the eyes—cold blue maggots devouring under glass. "For instance, I know all about Bennett's son Dolf. His hothouse, his flowers. He belongs in that hothouse because he's a hothouse pansy himself. And other hothouse pansies grow in the same bed with him. Understand? All it would take would be one little item in the paper. Factual. Substantiated by a vice-squad raid some dark night. Understand?"

"You bastard," said Corwin.

"In this instance, a term of affection. A compliment. And just remember, Corwin—" The cigar extended, cocked and aimed "—just remember that in this world the angels are trampled by the heels of bastards. Show me a real bastard and I'll show you a real winner. Every time! Always!"

"I've been shown," said Corwin. "So what are you driving at?"

Vollmer looked at his watch. "You want the Bennett layout, right?"

"Right."

"So you be over there at three o'clock sharp in his office with a check for one hundred forty thousand. He'll take it. I'll guarantee it."

The trouble was that Corwin believed him. It would happen just that way.

"I don't play this kind of game, Vollmer. I don't want the man crucified or intimidated for me."

"Neither one," said Vollmer. "Neither one. You have

my word. And, Corwin, if you don't buy at one hundred forty thousand, why then I'll know . . . I'll know—"

"You'll know what?"

Vollmer smiled. He crossed to the door. "Why, I'll know that you really never intended to buy Bennett's in the first place." He opened the door.

"Miss Kennedy. Be a good girl and show Mr. Corwin how to find the elevator, will you?"

Chapter 10

Todd Corwin didn't go to see Bennett personally. But at three o'clock sharp he was on the phone.

"Mr. Bennett, this is Todd Corwin."

"Yes," Bennett whispered.

"Have you thought over my offer, Mr. Bennett?"

"Yes."

"And what have you decided, sir?"

A good ten seconds went by. "Mr. Bennett, are you there?"

"I—I have been—I will accept a hundred and forty thousand."

"Good, good!" Oh God! It couldn't be worse.

"But I want to tell you, Mr. Corwin, that I—I am not at all happy with the deal. I accept reluctantly and only because—uh—certain pressures force me to do so. I think you must realize—I think you know very well that you're taking advantage of me."

Oh, Christ. The poor broken bastard. "Well now, Mr. Bennett, you don't have to sell if you don't want to."

"You know better than that."

"I never wanted to take advantage of you, Mr. Bennett. I have just so much capital to expend and that's it."

"Very well, very well. But I told you I would allow you a very substantial mortgage." Bennett's voice rose to a hoarser whisper.

89

"True. But I have other mortgages, other obligations. I can't go deeper in debt." God Almighty, what a farce!

"I'm sorry, Mr. Bennett."

There was another pause. "I understand that you—what time will you be here with the check? I have to go out soon."

"Not so fast, Mr. Bennett. As I told you, I'll have to have an audit on your books before we can close the deal. I want my own man on it and I'll have to get him up here from Florida. That will take a little time."

"I see. Well, of course that would be satisfactory." Bennett sounded relieved. "But in the meantime, I make no promise to hold the property for you. Several people have been looking and naturally, I would accept a better offer."

"Naturally. And I wouldn't blame you. I'll take that chance."

"You're not as hard a man as you appear to be, Corwin. I think you've come under the wrong influence. I advise you to be careful. Good-bye."

Corwin listened on a dead line, shrugged and hung up. Vollmer had reached the old man in that tender spot. He wasn't surprised. He had expected it. On the other hand, Vollmer had guessed that he wasn't going to buy. Or had he been told? And by whom? No, it was impossible. No one knew but Whitlock. So Vollmer must have put some facts together. What facts? What had he given away so early in the game?

It was moving swiftly towards a flare-up. It was going to come out in the open. He had that feeling. It would be a relief, of course. But he wasn't ready yet. Not at all ready. He could only hope that the Bennett stall would seem logical, would satisfy Vollmer long enough.

But Vollmer was too shrewd. It might occur to him that the purchase could be made under a legal contract stating that the deal was subject to an audit in proof of Bennett's annual net profit.

The hell with it. He would have to move faster now, that's all.

One thing was certain. Julie had been about to work for the Longport *Daily News*. It only took a little imagination to see that this was how she made contact with the

Vollmers. So that when she accepted that ride she must have felt perfectly safe in the hands of her new employer or a member of his family. Either she was flattered, or she found it impossible to refuse.

But why, God in heaven, why should anyone want to kill Julie Steadman?

He was driving back to the beach house. He was going to get the gun from his suitcase. From now on he was going to have to carry it. He was going to have to sleep with it. They weren't going to catch him off-guard the way they did Gordy.

Gordy, Gordy! You poor dead lonely sonofabitch. Lonely? No. Because he had followed Julie. Or was it naive, idiotic nonsense to suppose they were together. The mawkish dream-hope of the bereaved.

He was approaching the beach house driveway. He was right on the thirty-five-mile speed limit. And yet the police car had swung out of a side street and was holding the distance, tailing a hundred yards behind. He was beginning to wonder now if it was a prelude, a cold war to unnerve him, scare him off with a show of force.

He made the turn, sank back and sighed. Vollmer property would be sacred. And he was a guest. But his mirror didn't lie. They were still behind, keeping the distance, moving with leisurely assurance.

Apparently there was no one around. He nosed the car into the empty garage and got out, hearing the sound of their tires on gravel as he did so.

There were two officers on the front seat, a third in back. The driver leaned out and beckoned him with an arrogant little wave. He went over. The officers in front were the same two who had followed him along Broadway. In back was Gifford. The sheriff he had noted at Vollmer's town house or whatever he called it.

"See your driver's license please, sir?" said the cop who had signaled him. He was one of those good-looking boys who knew it, who admired his own smart uniform, who loved his petty power.

Corwin produced the license, handed it over. "Can't remember breaking any traffic regulation, Officer," he said. "And I might add, you're now on private property."

The officer's eyes flicked up with brief insolence before

they dropped again to the license. "Florida issue," he mumbled and looked back over his shoulder. "Man's name is Todd Corwin, all right, Sheriff. He's our boy."

The sheriff nodded, rocked his long jaw. The officer turned back.

"You're a long way from home, aren't you, Corwin?" he said.

"Is that a crime?"

"It can be, my friend. Under certain circumstances it certainly can be. Yes, sir, I think you'll find you would have been better off down there with the coconuts and the Crackers." He handed back the license. "Now, why don't you hop in back with the sheriff and we'll take a little ride."

"No, thanks," said Corwin. "Much obliged. Some other time, maybe."

"Save the comedy, Corwin," said the sheriff. "And don't make me get out or you'll be sorry. You're under arrest."

"What for?"

"You'll be told. Just get in and shut up."

It was a small red-brick building in a very run-down section of town. There were no police cars about, there seemed to be no activity at all. The building was ancient, shoddy. It had a look of settling into the ground, as if in time it would submerge altogether. And no one would care.

They drove around back to a dusty unkept parking area and, as they pulled up, the sheriff spoke for the first time since the ride began.

"Used to be a drunk tank," he said. "Drunks and vagrants, a few street cookies and brawlers, the overnight type of character. Then, a while ago they built a new station house and jail. Sweet layout. Air-conditioned, clean offices, flush toilets in the cells. Very pretty. Someday they'll get around to tearing this one down. But it might take years the way things move around here. Years."

The three doors opened almost together and he didn't have to be told to get out. The sheriff did not seem to be an idle talker. So his little story had meaning. Corwin knew he was about to learn that meaning.

LAMENT FOR JULIE

The sheriff unlocked a back door. They passed over warped wood flooring down a corridor. Corwin looked into what must have been a couple of offices. The rooms were dusty and bare of furniture. The air was stifling, smelled of wood decay.

At the front of the building there was the long scarred prisoner's reception desk. Empty, of course. No one spoke. There was only the creak and clump of shoe leather on old wood. The hall bent right and narrowing, passed a single empty cell. Beyond this a heavy steel door which the sheriff opened, exposing a semicircle of railed stairs which fell distantly to a great dungeon of a room, high-walled, window-barred.

In the center of the room below there were two heavy wooden chairs. The two men who sat in the chairs smoking, rose as they descended, waited with impassive faces. One of the men was the detective chief Gail had called Wade Utterback.

The other was Floyd Whitlock.

Just below the stairs and to the right there was a large open-gated cell. It contained several bunks in tiers.

The dungeon jail room had a dank rancid odor suggestive of unwashed bodies and urine.

Utterback and Whitlock had removed their coats and Corwin saw that both wore side arms. When Corwin was face to face with Whitlock, he said, "Some night I'm gonna catch you alone, Whitlock. No playmates around. And then you'll wish you never crossed me, you yellow sonofabitch."

Whitlock was fast. One big open hand fell like board across the side of Corwin's face. The other was a fist fired deep into his gut, doubling him. He remained bent, even after the pain left him. But when he came up, every ounce of his power came with him, all of it in the right smashing against the side of Whitlock's jaw.

Whitlock spun back, his knees collapsed and he went down.

The two uniformed cops rushed him then. But the waiting hate inside him had risen and they were toy soldiers. He belted one in the mouth, locked his fingers behind the other's head, brought the cop's face down

and kneed up into it. Then he ran. Up the stairs. Two,
three at a time, hurtled faster with great hand-pulls on
the railing.

The shot snapped past his head and pinged off the door
just as he was reaching for it. The shout followed hard
on the echo of gun blast.

"The next one will kill you, Corwin!"

He slammed against the door and stopped. Gulping for
air, he turned. Sheriff Gifford was at the foot of the stairs
holding a very steady .38 police revolver. Slowly, Corwin
went back down.

The sheriff did not look angry. There was even a hint
of respect in his eyes. The two patrol-car cops, staring
at him from bloody faces, would like to have murdered
him. Utterback watched him without expression. Whitlock
came out of the chair where he was holding his jaw, test-
ing it for breakage. He had a sap in his hand and was
lifting it, moving in. Utterback shot out an arm to stay his
progress.

"I wouldn't kill him, Wade," said Whitlock, disappointed. "Just let me ruin his nose and bash his mouth in."

"I might let you have him for a while later," said Utterback, breaking the cement of his features with a grin and
taking Corwin by the arm, leading him toward a chair.

Corwin swiped the arm loose. "Hands off," he warned,
and sat down.

"I'll get my boys cleaned up," said the sheriff. "They're
a goddamn disgrace. Back in ten minutes, Wade. I'll lock
the door behind me. And Wade—talk to him and that's
all for now. Understand?"

"Don't worry," Utterback said. "You run the county
and I'll run the city, Sheriff."

"You don't run anything but a bureau," said the sheriff
coolly. "And this is still a county case. Remember?"

"You know who runs them both," said Utterback with a
lazy smile.

The sheriff's lips tightened but he said nothing. He gave
the two battered cops a disdainful glance. "C'mon you
cotton-weights. I'm gonna work you both out in the gym
tomorrow. And I'll take you together."

They went up and out. There was the heavy sound of a
bolt closing.

LAMENT FOR JULIE

"Now listen you," said Utterback in the silence which followed. "That goddamn door up there is sealed shut but these guns are open for business. You may be a tough bimbo but I think I could handle you myself without a gun. And I'd like to try it. So don't give me any more trouble."

Corwin sized him up. He looked like plenty of fight, at that. He had shoulders like a truck radiator and biceps like one of those Italian construction workers. A big square face and ruthless brown eyes. The mostly quiet ones like Utterback and the sheriff would be dangerous in a scrap.

Whitlock stood by rubbing his jaw and staring malevolently.

"All right, what is it you want with me?" said Corwin. "This is strictly illegal and you know it. Charge me with something or let me go."

"We could charge you with murder and make it stick," said Whitlock. "And we will, sonny boy."

"If he opens his trap again, I'll shut mine for keeps," said Corwin, pointing at Whitlock. "You'll be talking to a wall. I mean it."

"He means it," said Utterback with a chuckle. "He knows from nothin' about how we could make him talk. But okay, to save time I'll unwind him myself, Floyd."

Whitlock grunted.

"Now," said Utterback. "Why did you come to this town, Corwin?"

Utterback was leaning over him, his face close. Over his shoulder, there was movement. Corwin's eyes drifted up and to his amazement he saw that behind the detective chief, Whitlock was closing one eye in a definite wink and giving his head a small negative shake.

"C'mon," said Utterback. "Why did you come here?"

"I came to deal with Bennett. I wanted to buy his anchorage if I could get a price on it."

"Nuts! You live in Florida. So how would you know anything about Bennett?"

"A friend told me he heard that Bennett was pressed and I could get a bargain."

"A friend? Would that be Gordon Steadman?"

Corwin saw that Whitlock was nodding vigorously.

95

"That's right," he answered. "I got a call from him about Bennett."

"You got a call from him, did you? Crap! You were right here in town and you were playin' around with his wife while he was away. She gets pregnant and you've had it with her, so you tell her to get off your neck. She threatens you. She's gonna tell Steadman, wreck you any way she can. You have a fight out on a lonely road and you kill 'er. You run 'er down. There's your phone call, buddy!"

Corwin was too astonished to speak. It took him a while to say, "That's a goddamn lie, you crawling bastard! You know how she died. You know who killed her. You tell me!"

"And then," Utterback went on blandly, "you beat it down to Florida, nice and cozy. Meantime, Steadman comes back, his wife is dead and he don't believe it's a simple hit-run. He finds out you were here and he suspects the whole lousy game. So he calls you and asks you to come up from Florida and give him a hand. Maybe he tosses in the Bennett deal for sauce, but anyway you can't refuse or you become guilty as hell in Steadman's eyes. And maybe he'll call cop on you. So you hop a plane and when you get to Steadman's house, he accuses you point-blank. And, brother, that's when you let him have it and make it look like suicide."

"Marvelous," said Corwin. "Oh, you're a wonder boy, Utterback. You should write for television."

"And finally," said Utterback, "you get hold of Whitlock here. Why? Because Steadman told you he was in touch with Whitlock and you're afraid Steadman spilled the beans about what he suspects. So you have to cover up—pretend you want to help in finding what you call the real criminal. And with that, my boy, the state rests its case."

"And where does the state get its proof?" asked Corwin.

"The state only needs to convict you of one murder, so the state tries you for the murder of Gordon Steadman. Proof? We have the weapon. A thirty-eight we'll manage to trace right back to you."

"Fantastic," said Corwin.

LAMENT FOR JULIE

"The trouble is," said Whitlock solemnly, "a jury would believe it and convict you."

Corwin could see that Whitlock was perfectly serious.

"I'll tell you something else," said Utterback. "A man could sit here in this hole for a week without food and water, living in his own stink, and I'll lay odds he'd sign a confession. No one would have to lay a hand on him."

"So this is Vollmer's idea of a reverse twist," said Corwin.

He and Wade Utterback stared at each other. And then the door opened and Sheriff Gifford came down the steps. Alone.

"Did you give him the word, boys?" he asked.

"He's got the picture," Utterback said.

"All right," said Gifford. "Wait upstairs a few minutes, Wade, take Whitlock with you."

Utterback looked at Whitlock and shrugged. They left. The sheriff drew up a chair, folded his legs. He took a pack of cigarettes from his pocket and offered one. Corwin refused. Gifford snapped a lighter and puffed.

"Don't try to beat this game, son," he said softly. "You can't. I've seen others buck the system and go down begging."

Corwin laughed bitterly. "What do you want me to do, sign a confession?"

"It might come to that. And it might not. You've got a choice. You can stand trial or—"

"Or what?"

"There's a plane leaving at ten o'clock tonight. You can be on it. You go home and you try to forget this thing. But forget it or not, you don't come back. Ever."

"Is that the choice you gave Gordon Steadman?"

"Something like that."

"And when he didn't get out, you killed him."

Gifford smiled—a slow, sad smile. "No, I didn't kill him."

"But you ordered it done."

"No, I didn't order it done."

"But you know who did it."

"You won't believe me, but I don't even know that."

"I'll bet you could guess."

"A guess wouldn't be good enough, Corwin."

97

"In my case, you know damn well I had nothing to do with it."

The sheriff was silent.

"And yet you're willing to frame me?"

"Under certain circumstances and for certain reasons you know nothing about, yes."

"You don't really look the type, Sheriff. Isn't there anyone in the entire police department, city or county, with an ounce of integrity? With even a half ounce of personal pride and decency?"

The sheriff studied the tip of his cigarette. "The answer might surprise you, Corwin. You remember the old saying—if you can't lick 'em, join 'em? Well, I take it a step further. I say if you can't lick 'em, join 'em until you can. Understand?"

"Are you speaking for me or for yourself, Sheriff?"

"Both, son. Both."

"Do you know anything about the circumstances of Julie Steadman's death?"

"Practically nothing. Nothing I can use."

"Why are you afraid of Vollmer, Sheriff?"

The sheriff stared calmly at him a moment, got up. "I think that's all, Corwin." He looked at his watch. "I'm going to give you an hour to make your choice." He turned and walked off, up the stairs and out.

There was the sound of the door being bolted home.

In twenty minutes the door opened again. It closed and was bolted from the other side. Whitlock came down the stairs carrying a brown paper bag. There was a thin smile on his face. As he approached he kept looking at Corwin warily to see if he had understood.

"My God, how did you ever do it?" Corwin said to relieve him.

"Keep your voice down, boy," said Whitlock, and handing him the paper bag, fell into a chair. "Burger and coffee. It was the sheriff's idea and I volunteered to bring it down. A good Joe, the sheriff. Mixed up, confused, but a very good Joe."

Corwin sipped the coffee, unwrapped the hamburger and took a bite. "Thanks, Floyd. For this and for the clues over Utterback's shoulder. Now, what's the story?"

LAMENT FOR JULIE

Whitlock flamed a cigarette. His hand shook. He touched his jaw. "Christ, you could have killed me. Sorry I had to poke you, but to a guy like Utterback, it looked good. Now I'm really on the team. All right, so I've got about ten minutes to play with while Wade is feeding his face with the sheriff. The other two cops are up there waiting, but they know from nothin'. They just do as they're told. Questions?"

"A hundred, Floyd. How did you get back on the force?"

"I can thank Gifford. It was his idea. Last night I got a call from him and we arranged a meet. Secret. I had to duck a tail. I'll cut it short. Gifford is basically an honest cop. He went along with Vollmer on hushing the Lansky information about the Caddy because he thought it was an accident, at first. And because the Lanskys beat it and there was no evidence anyway. To say nothing of an election coming up. And he could do more good in office than out.

"But then after your friend Gordy Steadman got it, Gifford knew it was murder. That suicide crap was for the papers. Hell, there were a half dozen clues made it clear what had happened—but not who did it. Then the sheriff was sure they were both murders, one covering the other. But he kept quiet, looking for an angle to nail Vollmer. He didn't know who to trust. Utterback's a grafter, so is his boss, the chief. So Gifford thought of me. He knew why I got canned, and he called me."

"Well, if he's county, how could he do anything for you in the city?"

"He couldn't, really. But he knew what was goin' on. He told me that they had a watch on me from an apartment across the street. They saw you come and go the first day and right off they traced back and found you were a friend of the Steadmans. They let you have a free hand to see what you would do. All this on Vollmer's orders, naturally. Utterback reports to him night and day. He don't know what he's hiding exactly, or why. But he takes orders.

"Anyway, the sheriff's idea was this. As long as they knew I was in contact with you, as long as they had the whole thing more or less figured, why not have me pretend

99

to play ball. I could play it for a change of heart, saying I knew I had pulled a dumb goof and wanted to make up for it. I would then give Utterback all the information he already knew, plus a few phony tips of my own. After which, they might put the mat out for me again. Then I could work from the inside.

"And it came off. Utterback fell for it and put me back on the job. I couldn't locate you anywhere on the phone and I didn't dare hunt you in person. But listen, that woman, the Keeler dame next door to Steadman, she was told to report anything that went on. She didn't know who you were, but she phoned in right after you left. Gave a description of you and the car, even had the license number. Gifford and Utterback were together at the time and Gifford offered to have you tailed. He wanted his hand in. Later he picked you up—same reason. That's about it. Except that Vollmer told Utterback to get rid of you one way or the other, even if he had to frame you. Gifford pretends to go along with it. He has to for the time being."

"I don't understand," said Corwin, "how the city and county divisions both got mixed up in it."

"Well, of course, they work together. But Mrs. Steadman was killed across the city line and Gordon Steadman in the city itself."

"And none of the cops on either force know a goddamn thing about who killed the Steadmans or why, Floyd?"

"Well, naturally, they suspect someone in the Vollmer clan. Or someone in Vollmer's pay. My God, you'd have to be an idiot . . . But if they know anything else, they're keeping their mouths shut. Gifford certainly knows no more than we do. Who can tell about Utterback?"

"What do we do now, Floyd?"

"I know what you'd better do. You'd better get the hell out of town and let us handle it. Because, boy, I'm not kidding, they can nail you with a fake story and fake evidence so fast you wouldn't know what happened to you. Why, for chrissake, you'd be punished for the very crimes you were tryin' to uncover."

"What about the Lanskys?"

"No time for details, but I traced them. They're in Europe somewhere, living it up. Not a chance with them."

"Well, I'm not leaving, Floyd. I just can't do it."

Whitlock flipped his cigarette across the floor, stood up. "Now wait a minute, boy. Just think a minute. In the first place you're no good, even to yourself, in this can."

"Right. So I'll say—Sure, I'll leave. And then I'll stay."

Whitlock ground his teeth, leaned over Corwin's chair. "You wouldn't get away with it. Remember your pal, Steadman? He was told to get out. And he didn't. And they killed him. Now listen to me—it could happen to you. Goddamn right. It could happen to you!"

"Maybe. Then I'll get on the plane. It's got to be a local. I'll get off at the first stop and fly back."

Whitlock was thoughtful. "It might work. You'd have to be goddamn sneaky and you'd have to hide out. Dangerous business if they catch you. I don't suppose you'd trust me and Gifford to wrap it up?"

"It isn't a matter of trust. Of course, I trust you. I've got to trust someone. But unless you could look inside my head and see what's swarming around in there, you wouldn't understand why I've got to do it myself."

"I give up," said Whitlock. "Boy, I'm sorry for you. I'm afraid for you." From his wallet he produced a card, crossed something out, flipped the card over and wrote. "Here. Keep this on you. You get in trouble, that's Gifford's office and home phone. You know how to reach me."

He stuck out his hand and Corwin shook it warmly.

"Now I'll go up and tell Utterback you're leaving on that plane." He looked at his watch. "It's right on to six o'clock. You got four hours."

101

Chapter 11

The taxi ground up the Vollmer beach-house drive. Corwin paid and got out. The taxi went off. He began to walk around the house. He was immeasurably tired. He was soul-deep sick of the whole brutal orgy of lies and counterlies, secrecy, violence—death. He wanted to go home and get back into routine. He wanted to be among friends. He felt utterly alone.

He didn't see a sign of anyone. But the garage door was closed and he paused, glanced into the little window. There was a car next to his rented Buick. It was the red Cadillac. It squatted there, long and full of sleek power and beauty. It seemed to breathe. It seemed a living thing. He had a wild impulse to find some kind of club and beat it into a shambles. Beat it to death!

He rounded the house and went up the stairs. He reached in his pocket for the key and with the other hand tried the door. It was open

He went in.

She was sitting in a chair across from the door, looking up at him with a strange expression. Something complex and fearful was in her face.

"Hello, Gail," he said.

"Todd. Oh, Todd. I've been waiting here for you." She got up and came toward him.

"How did you know I was coming?"

"I wasn't sure. But I knew that if you were—if you were leaving, you'd have to stop for your clothes."

"Oh? What makes you think I'm leaving, Gail?"

"I heard all about it," she said.

He studied her. She wore a magenta sweater and white skirt. Her black hair (he could only think of it as cool black) descended in clean brushed lines around the polished tan of her dainty well-bred face.

Cool. A smothering, torpid evening in July and yet from black crown to toe, as in the heat of a tennis

102

game, she looked immutably fresh and cool. Cool on the outside. Exterior insulation from the burning within.

"So you know all about it," he said.

"Yes. I got it from Warren Grimm."

"Warren Grimm? He of the second family to the Vollmers? How would he know?" Corwin moved about restlessly, settled on a stool of the little bar, looked at his watch. Six forty-five. "I would think you would get such news from dear old Dad."

"Dad? Huh! He tells me nothing. No one in the family tells each other anything. It's a dreary tomb of secrets. But my brother has a way of finding out things and he tells Warren. And Warren tells me. In a way, Warren is my best friend. Better than any girl I ever knew. Once we were sort of puppies together. But then we grew up and became . . . what? Close in spirit, I guess."

She came over and touched his cheek with a cool hand. "I've been worried about you."

"Oh, have you? Would you pour me a drink? On the rocks. Make it long and double it."

Frowning, she went behind the bar. "I can understand how you would need a drink."

"Can you now? Tell me, what did you hear?"

"That you were being held incommunicado in jail. That they were going to convict you of a certain crime if you didn't leave town." She slid the drink across to him and he downed half of it, coughed, wiped his mouth with the back of his hand.

"I don't suppose you know what crime they were talking about?" he said.

They went into the same lock-eyed silence of their last parting.

"I'm waiting," he said.

"You were a very close friend of—of Gordon and Julie Steadman, weren't you?"

"That's no answer."

"And you—you came here to get revenge."

"On whom?"

"On—" She looked down biting her lip. "On us," she whispered. "On the Vollmers."

"Oh? Why on the Vollmers? What have they got to do with the Steadmans?"

103

"I don't know—exactly."

"Sure you do." He drank. "I see you brought the red convertible. I thought it was too gaudy for your taste."

"The other cars were all busy." She moved to the sofa and sat down.

"You told me Joy was the only one who ever used that particular car."

Her head came up, her look was defiant. "I never said that! We all use it once in a while."

"Well, of course, it isn't important anyway." He crossed the room to stand over her. "Is it?"

"No. It's not in the least important."

"If it isn't important, why does it upset you?"

She didn't answer.

"You want me to tell you? Because that was the car that killed Julie Steadman. Wasn't it?"

She didn't answer.

His hand shot out and grabbed a mass of that cool black hair. He pulled back until she was forced to look up into his eyes. "Wasn't it?"

"You're hurting me."

"Wasn't it? Wasn't that the very same car!"

"I don't know, I don't know! Please—you're hurting me."

He held on. He wanted to slap the truth out of her.

"All right," she said. "All right!" she screamed. "It was the same car."

He let go. Smoothing her hair in place with nervous little dabs, she began to cry softly. "I never wanted to drive it again," she gulped. "I never wanted to touch it. But the others were gone and I had to get out here."

"You make me sick," he said. "All of you. You make me want to puke. Who fixed the fender? Who did the paint job on it?"

"I don't know." Fingers wiped under her eyes. "It could have been Tony, it could have been anyone. I heard hammering in the garage but the doors were closed, so I couldn't see."

"Who was driving the car that night?"

She looked up. "You're not going to believe me."

"No. But at this point I'll even listen to lies. Who was driving?"

"I'm not sure. And that's the truth. I don't really know."

He looked at his watch. He drank. "Why don't you know?"

"Because I had a date and he picked me up in his own car."

"What time did you get home?"

"Early. About ten. I had been out the night before and I was tired. Everyone was gone. The cars, too. Except the limousine."

"How would you know that—about the cars? Unless you made a point of looking?"

"I—I checked, I guess. How can I remember anything when you talk to me like a—a district attorney?"

"Where was your father?"

"I don't know. He never says where he's going."

"And your brother—Matt?"

"He was supposed to go somewhere with Warren Grimm. But then Warren had to stay over at the paper. So Matt said something to Joy about going with him to see the new floor show at the Starlite Casino. Matt was strange. He seemed preoccupied, nervous. At the time I thought it had something to do with Joy. But now I wonder if—Oh, what nonsense! You've got me suspecting everyone. Matt couldn't harm anyone. He just couldn't!"

"Was Joy in the habit of going places with Matt instead of your father?"

Her face tightened, her eyes narrowed. "It wasn't unusual. Oh, no, not at all. They were very—I hate to use the word close, but—"

"What were they, then?"

"They—I can't say it."

"Yes, you can."

"All right. They were lovers!" she spat. "And still are, for all I know. Oh, that bitch. That evil, evil bitch!"

"Evil has two faces," he said. "Maybe she's not entirely to blame. Does your father know?"

"I'm not sure. He wouldn't tell me if he did. But one day I came down here unexpectedly and I—I caught them. Sick, sick, sick. Sickening!"

He was beyond surprise. He was silent, watching the play of emotion across her face.

105

"And now you want to know what I think, Todd? What I really believe it adds up to? Looking back, it seems to me that Matt was nervous because he was covering for Joy. Tht whole conversation between them about going to the Starlite Casino was strained. Joy sounded so false. As if she had some scheme, as if she were going someplace else and needed Matt for an alibi. She had a hold on Matt and he would do anything for her. He could even be blackmailed into it. So they pretended to be going out together. But instead, Joy takes the convertible and she drops Matt somewhere. And then she goes on by herself and she—well, anyhow, the point is that she must have been the one who was driving that car."

It was logical. Corwin could see that it might have happened just that way. And yet, when the Vollmers weren't lying for each other, they were lying about each other. He was in a torment of confusion.

"And where was Tony that night?" he asked.

"Tony? That brainless muscle? Another of Joy's love slaves. Of course I can't prove it, but—"

"Where was he?"

She shrugged. "He had a night off."

"So you don't know where anyone was exactly, what they were doing or which car they had?" He put down his glass and lit a cigarette. "That right?"

"Yes. Because, as I told you, I had a date and I left first."

"Does Tony ever take one of the family cars on his night off?"

"Only once that I can remember. He has his own jalopy. But it's possible."

"All right. You're innocent. Everyone is innocent. The car just drove off and killed Julie by itself. But the next morning you must have found out about it. How?"

"Why, it was in the paper. We ran a pretty big story. I didn't think much of it at the time. A perfect stranger killed by some drunk."

He fell into a chair, leaned toward her. "No mention in the paper implicating a Vollmer, of course."

"Naturally not. I'm sure there was nothing known at the time as to who might have . . ."

LAMENT FOR JULIE

"And no mention of the fact that Julie Steadman was going to work for the *News?*"

"No! And where did you hear that?"

"Never mind. Just tell me this. How could she have met anyone but your father at the paper if no one else in the family works there?"

"Oh," she gasped. "Is that your line of reasoning? Well, maybe we don't work there. But it's nothing unusual for us to drop by. Matt often hangs around Warren when he's working. Joy stops in to see Dad—when she wants something. And so do I. Tony waits there with the car when he's told to. But why would we introduce ourselves to Julie Steadman— a stranger? Pretty far-fetched, Todd."

"Maybe. But it has to begin somewhere. Let's get back to you. The first news about Julie Steadman you got from the paper. And that morning, where was the red convertible?"

"I don't want to talk about it any more, Todd. They're a pretty messy bunch, but they're my family. I have just a grain of loyalty left."

"Gail. Listen to me. Julie and Gordy Steadman were both murdered."

She shook her head. "It was an accident and a suicide."

"You don't sound convinced. You don't believe it. In fact, you know it wasn't an accident and a suicide. I know it. The police admit it. It was murder. If you did it, then just shut up. But if you didn't, don't talk to me about loyalty. Murder and loyalty don't mix."

She wet her lips. She stared at him. She wet her lips again. "That same morning," she said softly, "I was awakened by some pounding in the garage. I looked out the window. The garage doors were closed. I wondered why Tony would be working on one of the cars at that hour. I wondered why the doors were closed. But only for a moment. I went back to bed. The pounding stopped and I fell asleep. I had forgotten about it when I got up. I saw the convertible later in the day and it looked the same as ever.

"The story broke. But it wasn't a topic of discussion. Then the next evening when Dad came home, Sheriff Gifford was with him. Dad's face was a cloud, a big dark cloud ready to storm. He and the sheriff went into the study. They came out in about an hour and the sheriff left.

"Then Dad called us all together and he said, 'Which one of you took the convertible last night?' No one answered. He stared around at all of us in turn. Still, no one said a word. Then he told us to sit in the living room and he called us into the study one at a time. When it was my turn he asked me to account for the night before, where I went, how I got there, what I did, when I came home. He seemed satisfied. After all, I had the only decent alibi. Finally, he told me that witnesses saw the Steadman woman get into our car—the convertible. And they had reported it to the police. He said it was going to be kept quiet and nothing would come of it. But I was to tell him anything I could find out about the others.

"I waited and watched everyone come and go to the study—even Tony. Some took longer than others. And then it was over."

"What was their reaction?" Corwin asked.

"Well, everyone had been told not to discuss a word of what was said in private. And they didn't. They came out with blank faces and went their way. All except Joy. She didn't say anything, but I could see she had been crying. She went to her room. And that's all I know. But I couldn't get it off my mind. Especially when Mr. Steadman killed himself—or whatever."

"Or whatever," said Corwin. He got up and went into the bedroom. She followed him. He began to pack his clothes. Without haste. Deliberately. While his mind was elsewhere.

And all the time she sat on a corner of the bed and watched in silence. Even when he inspected the gun and put it in his pocket.

He was carrying the suitcase to the door when she stopped him. "Take me with you," she said. "Take me out of this nightmare town. Away from the horror of my own family. They're all bad. They're all evil. No strings. Just take me with you."

"I couldn't if I wanted to," he said. "And I don't."

"Will you kiss me good-bye?"

LAMENT FOR JULIE

"No."

"You did more than kiss me once."

"That was different."

"Why?"

"I had to open doors. It was business."

She slapped him.

"But now if I kissed you, I wouldn't have an excuse. It might be the dirtiest kiss of my life. Like kissing death. The death of my friends."

She slapped him again.

Then slowly her face crumpled. She seemed about to cry. "Oh, I'm sorry, I'm sorry I did that," she said. "You don't mean any of these things you're saying. Not really. It's because of the strain you're under."

"Is that so? Well, you just go right ahead and convince yourself, Gail."

"I only want to convince you," she said. And then her arms went around his neck and she pressed tightly against him, bending his head down and forcing her lips over his.

He tried to push her away but she clung to him desperately. And all at once, as if her nearness were hypnotic, he found himself washed of resistance. He pulled her roughly against him. And, returning the kiss fell free of his hate into a plunging velvet-soft forgetfulness.

Then he broke away and picked up the suitcase.

"So what does that little experiment prove?" he said. "Nothing! Except that when you bring two opposites together, by some goddamn stupid law of nature there's got to be a reaction. Mindless. Involuntary. I repeat, involuntary! So don't look for meaning where there isn't any."

"Oh, Todd, Todd! Why are you so driven? Why must you include me in all your hating?"

"Because you stand for all that I despise. Because your very name stinks of evil and treachery and death!"

But even as he said it, another part of him was wrenched by the pleading pathetic look of her. And he wanted to hold her again, to kiss and comfort her. To feel in the close weld of her body, the warm release from all that tortured him.

109

Instead, he opened the door and went out. He hurried down the stairs, not turning back, closing his mind and his heart to the sound of her voice calling after him.

Instead, he opened the door and went out. He hurried down the stairs, not turning back, closing his mind and his heart to the sound of her voice calling after him.

Chapter 12

He arrived at the airport in a taxi. He was over a half hour early because he wanted to establish his presence. Meanwhile, under an assumed name, he had checked in at a motel on the outskirts of town. He had been extremely watchful. No one had followed him. He had left the rented Buick at the motel.

The waiting room of the terminal was too bright and too muggy and too full of damp travelers. It seemed a sleepy place. Activity was in slow motion. Loudspeakers droned monotonously and no one stirred.

Corwin glanced about but could not recognize a single face. Yet secret faces watch undetected.

The clerk behind the counter inspected his ticket, weighed the suitcase and gave him the claim check without a single change of expression. There was a dreamlike quality to it all and he moved with a sense of unreality to a bench and sat down to wait. He found himself irritated that his departure would apparently go unnoticed.

And then someone sat down beside him and he felt the small nudge of an elbow. He turned his head. It was Warren Grimm. Gone was the pleasant smile and the self-complacent charm. The long strands of sandy hair were awry over the pale handsomeness of his features. He looked drawn, intent. Hands in his lap, tendril fingers entwined and fought each other. His eyes did not look at Corwin, but nervously scanned the room.

"I shouldn't be here, Mr. Corwin," he said in a hushed

110

voice, "I shouldn't be seen with you. If they think I'm taking sides—I don't know. Anything could happen. But I came to warn you. In case you tried anything foolish just because it looks so peaceful in here."

His head came around and their eyes met. A delicate, sensitive face—yet strong, somehow, shedding boyishness for maturity in a moment of stress.

"Listen to me, Mr. Corwin. Just listen, please. I haven't much time. They're outside. Waiting in the dark. Wade Utterback and Floyd Whitlock. And the sheriff. And three men I've never seen before. Strangers. They look like—I don't know. As if they were brought in from out of town for some purpose. Can't you guess? They're all watching the doors and the gate to the plane. I told Utterback I was to meet someone flying in and he gave me a very odd look. So I'd better—"

"Who sent you?" Corwin interrupted. "Gail?"

"Well—"

"I suppose she wants to make sure I get on the plane. Then she'll feel safe."

"No, sir, honestly. It's true that I talked to her. But she didn't send me."

"It doesn't matter," said Corwin, unconvinced. "I'm here, I'm leaving. It's over for me. What time does the celebration start? Five after ten?"

"Of course you're bitter." His speech came soft and rapid from the corner of his mouth. "And I understand why. But there's a lot more behind this than you can see. Factions within factions. High corruption and low corruption. And fear, always fear. The Steadmans were tragic catalysts for a much larger explosion to come."

Corwin couldn't withhold a wry smile. Grimm sounded like a walking editorial, full of wordy overdramatic prose, while a juvenile in real understanding. "I'm not interested in larger explosions," he said. "I just want to get out of this goddamn town and let it wallow in its own filth. Thanks for the tip, Grimm, but you'd better go before you find yourself without a job on that paper."

Grimm moistened his lips and shot his eyes into every corner. "For my health, Mr. Corwin. Not for the job. I'm going to work for my father. I'm going to quit the paper. I know too much that I can't stomach."

111

"Why do you hang around the Vollmers if you know so much, Warren?"

"Because when the right time comes I'm going to have a story to end stories."

"Who would print it?"

"The opposition. The *Bulletin*. And the wire services."

Corwin looked at him with new interest. "Do you know anything you want to tell me, Warren?"

Grimm shook his head. "No, sir. Not here and now. You'd never get on that plane."

"Now listen, Grimm. Don't play big time with me. Do you really know anything?"

"A guess, Mr. Corwin. A very well-educated guess. And so far from your own thinking, you wouldn't believe it. Just watch the papers wherever you are. Good-bye, sir. And luck."

"Grimm!"

But Warren Grimm didn't turn back. He moved across the floor with long strides, at once youthful and naive, ancient and wise with his fearful knowledge.

Corwin had never seen the gum-chewing man who watched the passengers through the gate with too casual an interest. And couldn't see into the shadows behind the field-skirting fence where he knew others peered with solemn satisfaction. And on the plane, all the tired faces were unfamiliar, yawning behind newspapers or asleep on the little white pillows brought by the stewardess with her professional smile, a soundless shadow bending and drifting up the aisle.

At the terminal in Washington, he made a show of checking the connection to Miami. Fifty minutes. He asked the clerk a question and the clerk picked up a phone and called somewhere.

Yes, the clerk said, it was still possible to charter a plane to most anyplace.

He sauntered in many false directions—the men's john, the newspaper stand, the bar, always watching. All the faces of all the people were disinterested. Finally there was the fresh-air stroll with little pauses and natural turnabouts.

No one at all.

In a few minutes he was seated in the office of the

charter company and the man was circling a pinhead area on a map. It was a town about fourteen miles distance from Longport. A small plane could land on the tiny field. An hour and twenty minutes flying time.

He gave the porter a dollar and the claim check for his suitcase. He waited in the office for the plane to be readied.

At ten minutes after one a.m., the taxi planted him in front of the Longport motel where he had his room. The Buick sat undisturbed in the space before his door. He gave the key a twist and went in, checking the blinds before giving the room light.

He tossed the suitcase into a closet and sat on the bed with a sigh. He sucked in deep breaths of cool air, for he had left the conditioner running. He was no longer tired. He was far too tense. It had gone well enough. Or if not, he would soon know. There remained a final action. Something direct but necessarily dangerous. No more time for subtlety. He could only move at night, and then with caution. And how long could he hide, even under the best conditions?

He stared at the phone. The motel office was dark, the No Vacancy sign up. The guy would be asleep. He wouldn't be able to place a call through the switchboard.

He stepped outside and went to the public booth. He dialed Whitlock's number, reading from the scrap of paper he took from his wallet.

A woman's voice inquired sleepily. "Tell him it's Corwin," he said.

Whitlock came on with the sound of a man already divorced from sleep. "Where are you?"

"At a motel in town."

"Jesus!"

"I want action, Floyd. Tonight."

"Oh, Christ. You may get the wrong kind."

"You were at the airport, I hear. You think I got away with it? Or did they figure me to flip back again?"

"They figured you for the kind of guy who wouldn't leave at all unless he was convinced for keeps. But for the time being they put a twenty-four-hour watch on incoming transportation. How the hell did you sneak by?"

113

"Chartered a plane to a field no bigger than Vollmer's lawn and twice as rough. Then taxied in."

"Smart."

"Listen, Floyd. You have anything at all on Vollmer good enough to bring 'im in for a sweat?"

"Are you crazy, man?"

"Nope. How about that gun? The one that killed Gordy."

"Bought locally. Guy who sold it says he can't remember the buyer. But I don't believe it and I'm gonna keep workin' on the bastard."

"So that leaves what? The red convertible. Since Vollmer has all the cars in his name that makes him primarily responsible. The car could be impounded as evidence with help from Sheriff Gifford."

"What evidence? A repainted fender? So his boy Tony says it got dented when he put it in the garage one night."

"I know. We need more. What I want to do is get into that garage and look around. It's a hundred to one. But I might just find something that would tie in. It wouldn't take much. A scrap of cloth from Julie's dress, a few hairs, anything like that."

"My God! If they caught you, I couldn't help you one bit. Gifford couldn't show his hand, either."

"Sure, sure. But I have to try it. You wanna come along?"

"When?"

"Now."

Silence. "I'll tell you, kiddo. I'd give my tail for ten minutes in that garage. But—and don't think I'm yellowing out on you—I don't think it's a good idea. Look at it this way. If I got caught, that would finish me in the department. And there goes your inside track. No more drool from the horse's mouth. See what I mean?"

"Right. I agree. So I'll give it a whirl myself."

"I wish you wouldn't."

"Got to. Can't sit still any longer, Floyd."

"Oh, Christ, be careful. And call me after. Okay?"

"First instant, Floyd. See you."

"Luck, Todd."

He went back into the room and checked the automatic.

114

He fed a round into the chamber and put the gun in his pocket.

He backed the Buick and quietly slid down the drive to the road.

He hadn't an inkling that anything was wrong. The road was deserted, the gun was in his pocket, he felt good. He had this conviction that he was going to get in the garage without being discovered, that he was going to find some damning little piece of evidence with which to impale Austin Vollmer.

And the headlights splayed from the side road, bent his way in the rear-view mirror and shot after him with that purposefulness which is unmistakable trouble.

That made him pretty goddamn nervous but it didn't kill his spirit altogether. He could drive. He was good behind a wheel. He had some distance and anyway they weren't going to get abreast to force him over. If there was a wreck, it wasn't going to be the Buick.

And the gun was still in his pocket.

So he stepped down hard on the pedal and found that his rental still had some guts. He was chewing up road and they were coming, but not fast enough. It now became a matter of tight maneuvering, escape and a change of plans. With luck, not much more.

This was his night and they weren't going to take it from him.

It had never occurred to him to check the back seat or the floor below it. And now it was too late because the gun barrel was cool against his neck and the guy was saying,

"Just about forty will do it. You hold 'er there, buddy, because we wouldn't wanna get arrested, now would we? And let me see hands. Both of 'em on the wheel. That's it. Now we'll just cruise along here for about another half mile and then we'll cut right when I tell you. Meantime, keep your mouth shut and drive this heap at forty per."

He didn't turn around. He had the feeling it would be unwise. The barrel slid along his skin, dug in obliquely behind his ear and stayed there. He could tell they

115

weren't going to play with him. They weren't going to take chances. The whole setup had the air of calculated smoothness and perfection of detail—a professional killing in the works.

He was not merely frightened. His mind was almost in total erasure with terror.

He did think desperately of the two possibilities. A quick hand to the pocket for the gun. Ridiculous! A wrench of the wheel and off the road, the bastard with the gun thrown off balance, the element of surprise in his favor. Stupid! Because in the mirror, the other car wasn't a hundred yards behind.

He had to say something. He needed the reassuring sound of his own voice. And what could he lose? He made it brave and casual. "Sure would get a kick out of knowing how you found me," he said, surprised that the interior shaking didn't rattle his voice.

"I told you to be a clam. But okay, punk, you got one answer comin'. When you didn't turn this load in at the rental joint, we were wise. We got the dope on the Buick, plates, year, color and we started checkin' around. We figured you for a motel and the rest was easy. Satisfied? Then close your goddamn face and haul right at the next crossroad."

It could have been five minutes or ten. He had no sense of time. But toward the last there was an awareness that he had been ordered to turn onto a familiar road. He couldn't tell why it was familiar in the darkness until they came to a bridge and passed over a stream. The road was a narrow blacktop rising under the headlights between thick woods on either side.

This was the road on which Julie walked to her death. Unless she was already dead when the car struck her. No, she must have been upright when the fender caught her.

Once he had come to this place—half in morbid curiosity, half in the feeble hope of finding some clue. He had dreaded the possibility of stumbling upon some nauseous physical evidence of her death. But there had been nothing. Not even a twisted shoe or a torn stocking.

Whitlock had told him how to fix the exact spot by a white stake driven in the weeds beside the road. He knew they weren't far from the stake when the gun barrel gave him a little jab and he was ordered to swing left.

At first he couldn't see any sense to it. There wasn't anything there. But he braked and saw the narrow edge of dirt road which dipped down into the trees. He made the turn and they were swallowed by infinite darkness, the trees nearly closing overhead to make a tunnel of green. Behind them the lights of the other car fell and rose again.

He kept thinking now of his own stupidity. Why didn't he make some move—any move? Why prolong it? But the gun never left his head and his brain was numb with probing for a single decent plan.

"Okay, jerk. Stop here in this clearing and wait. Cut the lights."

He obeyed. The lights behind winked out. They sat in darkness.

Figures approached softly. Two men behind a flash.

"Get out."

He did.

He could see now that two of them were big men. Tall, at least. The one with the flash was almost a head shorter. All wore masks. Black, eye-slitted cloth tied around the face. Dark shirts and dark trousers. Even then, he was struck by the absurdity of it. If they were going to kill him, why did they mask their faces? Perhaps an extra precaution. In case he got away and remembered. But how unlikely!

Three men. The three strangers at the airport mentioned by Warren Grimm?

The one who had been just a voice behind him, shoved him forward. He had the most size and seemed to possess the only gun. They moved in silence over a narrow twisting path. In the moonlight he could see the shadowy outline of a misshapen shack ahead. It leaned and sagged in disconsolate abandonment. The sound of moving water grew upon them. He remembered the bridge and the stream. Cool water on a night swollen with heated air. The clean smell of things growing and the dank smell of rotting. And the intolerable weight of fear.

Hands turned him roughly and pushed his back flat against the crude boards of the shack. They grouped

117

around him in black silence, looking grotesque behind their masks. The broad-chested one with the gun and the look of sleek muscle-power and agility, held the weapon so the barrel looked up into Corwin's face.

"You want me to do it?" he said to the others.

They didn't answer.

"Alex, you wanna finish 'im?"

"No," said the other tall one. In that one word, there was both disdain and command.

"Wally?" This to the shortest. "Don't let me hog the fun."

"He's yours," said the one called Wally. His voice, like the others, had youth but not hardness. A nervous rasp, in which was painted the most dreadful picture of all, as if the owner of the voice might later be sick.

The holder of the gun, standing dip-shouldered, easy and relaxed, chuckled. "You never did like blood, Wally. You could wait in the car."

Wally said nothing.

Something about this big one with the gun, his stance and manner, even the look and sound of him touched on a memory. But Corwin's brain spun in a crazy pattern of confused impressions and there was no importance to anything but escape and survival. He did not speak because all effort was coiled and waiting for the precise moment of greatest chance. Besides, there was nothing to say.

As if a signal had been given, the tall one called Alex stepped up beside the one with the gun and extended his arm until the arms of each man were parallel. And now both held the gun and it came to Corwin that for some insane reason of shared responsibility or sadism, they would pull the trigger together. But then nothing happened except that the gun changed hands without actually being passed from one to the other. A practiced arrangement.

None of it made sense. They hadn't even searched him.

Now the heavy-chested nameless one who had touched his memory, drew gloves from his pocket. The gloves looked as black as the masks. He began to pull the gloves on, working them carefully over his fingers. He came close while Alex held the gun and the short figure did nothing but stand and shift.

"Thought you were a dead one, didn't you, lover-boy?" Gloved fingers still kneading each other. "Nah. Too risky and no fun. You're only gonna be half dead. Broken. Mouth, nose, jaw. Broken. Legs, arms, fingers. Broken. You get out of the hospital inside three months, you're a lucky sonofabitch. You come back again—" Gloved finger extended, thumb cocked. "—bang! Right through the head."

He saw the blow coming in that split second. But he couldn't duck fast enough. It caught him on the cheekbone, spun his head and rammed on into the board with a force that told him his face was going to be ripped to pieces. He felt the thin board shake and give behind him and something crossed his mind, went dim with the kidney punch, faded in the rattle of his skull from the blow to his head, the hammering of his jaw, the blasting of his eye.

Blood ran into his mouth and, with the taste of it, he let himself sag forward, head bent. Numbly he felt blows, saw feet. Suddenly he stepped out, turned sideways and rammed back with his shoulder. Two hundred rockpounds of man splintered the rotting boards and he fell through to the floor.

He remembered to keep moving and rolled himself to a dark corner. The gun was barely in his hand when the first shadow destroyed light from the splintered opening. He fired with absolute intention to kill but without time to ready his aim. The shadow ducked back with astonishing speed. Likewise, the figure looming in the doorway disappeared as he brought the gun around.

In the silence he heard low voice and harsh whisper. He could imagine the change of heart the sound of his gun had brought about. He waited. All was quiet. Too long a quiet. Not a rustle. Then he heard the motor sound and the whine of backing.

He flew out and down the trail to the road. They were backing without lights and the sound was diminishing, though he could see outline. He fired twice, carefully. Wildly they returned his fire and he hit the ground.

Then they were gone.

119

He ran to the Buick. No keys. They had taken them. He was surprised they had thought of it. There was, after all, something not quite so professional about the job. The shaky voice of the shorter one. The overdramatic, too clever switching of the gun.

Now they would wait for another time. But there wouldn't be another.

He reached in his pocket for cigarettes, found them. And also the keys! It came back to him. Habit. Unbreakable even in the utmost stress. He had taken the keys from the switch. Automatically.

Too late to hurl after them. And foolish, with the odds three to one. He turned the car around and then sat there with the motor idling. He was sweating and yet he was cold. He began for the first time to tremble in little spasms. Now he became aware of the blood drooling from the side of his face, down his neck and into his collar. His face felt dead, the way his lip did after the dentist's needle.

He got out a handkerchief and mopped gingerly. The flesh around his cheekbone was gouged open, eye and jaw puffed and raw. Nose and mouth okay. Still trembling, he smiled. He was very glad to be alive.

Now he sat very still and, with that special talent he had for total recall, relived the experience. Not the pain, fear or shock, but the look of the men. Especially the glove-and-gun bastard. The way he appeared, slouching there. The way he talked and moved.

He discarded the voice. If ever he had heard it before, it could only have been for a moment. No, forget voice, but recall attitude, stance, build. Keeping the picture in frame he went over everyone he had met since his arrival, attempting to superimpose one image over another. Slowly, by a process of association and elimination, he swept away all the images but one.

Then he flared the lights and gunned back to the highway.

Chapter 13

The Vollmer house was just a great dark blob way up on top of the hill between the ranks of trees. He had the lights out long before he reached the driveway. He parked the car and hiked to the big iron gate set in the wall. The gate was locked. Naturally. Vollmer should have more than walls and gates. He should have fortresses.

It was a small problem because he climbed a tree and made his way hand over hand from branch to wall, leaping down. Then he jogged over the grass up the hill. He tried the garage doors but found them locked. He toed around to the side and right away he saw the car standing there—a squat Ford sedan which dipped so low in back it seemed to be rearing from haunches. He felt the radiator. It wasn't warm. It was hot.

The stairs were in back and he took them noiselessly two at a time. Of course, the door was locked. But there was a window to the right, open against the heat. It was just out of reach so he had to leap and grab the sill. Not much of a sound but he listened a moment before hoisting himself in.

His eyes adjusted to a small cluttered living room. He groped down the only hall, past a kitchen to a door. A feeble dot of light appeared below it. Listening, he heard water and understood. He turned the knob slowly and went in with the gun in his fist.

Unmade bed, bureau, a table and chairs. A look of disorder and the damp rotting-apple smell of unwashed laundry. No light in the room but one behind the half closed door of a bath. He got to it without a sound and swung it open silently.

Tony, the chauffeur, was dressed in the black trousers of his uniform, though bare to the waist. The butt of a revolver was just visible over the rim of his hip pocket. Tony was drying his hands on a soiled towel while baring his teeth to the mirror, approving their whiteness. Black

121

hair sprouted over his heavy shoulders and even over the sinuous bulging of his arms.

He dropped the towel to the floor and smoothed the oily dark sideburns against his skull. As Corwin stepped forward his eyes changed in the mirror and the mass of his back became frozen.

"Just getting in, Tony-boy?" said Corwin.

Tony must have seen the gun in the mirror. He began to turn warily.

"Hold it, Tony!" Corwin reached out and plucked the revolver from Tony's pocket, dropped it into his own. "Now," he said.

Tony came around slowly with nervous eyes, though his face was pulled tight with bluff surliness. "So?" he said. "What you want?"

Corwin backed into the room and with a wave of the gun, beckoned Tony to follow. "Turn on a light, Tony."

Tony obeyed and Corwin walked over to the bureau, picked up black gloves and a slitted square of black cloth. He held them up.

"So what?" said Tony, standing hands on hips in the center of the room, moistening his lips.

"Hands okay, Tony-boy? Didn't hurt them on my face, did you?"

Tony didn't answer. His mouth hung open and on his face was the effort of ponderous thought.

"You're a brave, brave fighter, Tony. You can hit. I admire brave, brave fighters who can hit. Who were the others, Tony? Alex and Wally."

Tony shifted on his feet.

"You'll be telling me all about it, Tony. I figure you to hold out for another minute, maybe."

Corwin let the black square fall to the floor, laid the gun on the bureau and tested his fingers in one of the gloves. "About my size. Not a bad fit." He pulled the gloves on with deliberate care while Tony palmed his hair, his face, wondering if there was a chance in the world of some clever move before Corwin could get hold of the gun.

"Good gloves," said Corwin, smiling. "Not too heavy, not too light. Just right." He picked up the gun again. "You want this little shooter, Tony? Sure you do." He gave it a toss and it landed in the center of the bed where it lay with blue-black innocence against the white of rumpled sheets.

Tony looked at the gun, tensed, hesitated.

"Still worried? Oh, I get it, you're afraid of the other one." Corwin removed Tony's revolver from his pocket and pitched it like a quoit. It sailed neatly and landed with a clink on top of the automatic.

They moved almost together. Tony was fast. His hand was just closing on the top gun when Corwin chopped his temple and sent him reeling back to the floor. Tony got up holding his head, looking at his hand, wiping a smear of blood on his trousers. Corwin stood on the other side of the bed, working the gloves, waiting.

Tony tried again and this time Corwin caught him harder, just above the left eye. When Tony got up he didn't even look at the guns. He came around the side of the bed and stood crouched in the center of the room.

"That's a good stance, Tony. You'll go far with that. You'll make a brave, brave fighter."

Corwin was through playing with him. He moved in and gave the rock of his shoulder to Tony's first blow, jabbed the same eye with a left, took Tony's heavy right in the gut, danced aside, waited for the rush, danced again, feinted, found the precise moment and gave Tony all of it—the hate, the stone fist, the two hundred pounds in the mouth.

It was a lovely sound and the feeling was of much breaking and cutting, as if his fist were going to push through into Tony's throat. While Tony's forward motion came to a jerking halt, his head snapping back with a bright crimson grimace full of jagged holes where minutes before teeth had gleamed back at him in the mirror.

Corwin really wanted to stop then but couldn't find the switch and had to finish that bad eye, make a red mash of the nose and punish the chin. Of course, with Tony on the floor, a wet glob of busted features, it ended.

Then he grabbed Tony by the hair and pulled him to sitting position. Tony was sobbing, really weeping, coughing up teeth between sobs.

"You've still got half a face left," cried Corwin. "You wanna lose the other half?"

"Don't," Tony moaned. "Jesus God, no more," he gurgled.

"Quick, then! Who were the others? Wally and Alex."

"Wally is—they're—they're just names we made up. Wally is Matt—Matt Vollmer."

"And the other one?"

"I dunno. I swear to God, I dunno. He was with Matt and he had the mask on and Matt wouldn't tell me. It was part of the deal."

"What deal?"

"Matt give me five hundred to help with it, throw a scare into you."

"Who killed Julie Steadman?"

"I dunno nothin' about that."

"Who killed Gordon Steadman?"

Tony mopped his face with an already soaked handkerchief. "Listen, you gotta believe me. I thought Steadman knocked himself off. Whatever's been goin' on, I had nothin' to do with it. Mr. Vollmer, he paid me to fix the fender. He give me a grand to keep my mouth shut. He said it was an accident and it wouldn't do no good to spread it around. That's it. That's every bit of it, you gotta believe me. I was off that night and I never could find out. The car was in the garage next morning and Mr. Vollmer, he calls me in and tells me to fix it. Jesus, I was nearly sick. But after that I just did what I was told, what I got paid extra for."

"Sure," said Corwin disgustedly. "Just what you were told. We'll see about that. Where is Matt Vollmer now?"

"In his room."

"I want him over here. Fast! You'll see to it."

"I could phone the room," said Tony meekly. "I got a phone here connects all over the house."

"Do it! I'll listen. You make it sound right to me."

"Yes, sir." Tony got shakily to his feet. He saw a tooth on the floor, picked it up, examined it and began to cry.

"Shut up and get to that phone or you'll need a whole mouthful."

"Yes—yes, sir."

Corwin plucked the guns from the bed, put them in

his pockets. He followed Tony to the living room, leaving the door open for light. Tony slumped by a phone on the wall, examined buttons a moment and pushed one, lifting the receiver. He listened, pushed the button again.

"Matt?" he said in a low urgent voice. "Tony. We got trouble. You better come right over here. . . . No, I can't talk on the phone. Hurry it up, for God's sake." He hung up.

"That'll bring 'im," he said.

They waited in the semigloom. When they heard steps, Corwin stood back and Tony opened the door. The minute Matt Vollmer walked in, Corwin took two quick steps forward and smashed him in the face. He stumbled and fell with a meaty thud. Corwin got on top of him in a hurry and pinned knees to his arms. He got his hands around Vollmer's neck, thumbs at the windpipe. He began to apply pressure slowly.

Vollmer wiggled frantically without success. "Goddamn," he choked. "Goddamn, who are you?"

"I'm death," said Corwin. "I'm your death in thirty seconds unless I get the truth." He pressed tighter. Tony, holding his battered face, sat in a chair and watched in awe. "Did you kill Julie Steadman, you sonofabitch! Did you run that helpless girl down in that big car? Did you?" He banged the head on the floor.

"No, no." A feeble sound, breathless. "Let up, let up."

Corwin released pressure, Vollmer's eyes focused and recognized. "I didn't do it," he said. "I didn't!"

"Who did?"

"I don't know."

"Who was the one called Alex tonight?"

"I don't know that, either."

Corwin released him and he got up, rubbing his neck, "Tony," said Corwin, rising. "Come here into the light."

Tony came.

"Now, Vollmer, you take a good look at Tony's face."

Vollmer looked, winced, looked again. "Goddamn," he moaned.

"Open your mouth, Tony."

Tony opened painfully.

"He did that?" whispered Vollmer.

Tony nodded.

"You're gonna look a lot worse," said Corwin. "Why did you kill Julie Steadman?"

Vollmer turned. His eyes were enormous. "I didn't, I didn't!"

Corwin studied him. Vollmer was too small for the kind of beating he wanted to give. So Corwin took out his gun and pointed it at Tony. "Tony," he said. "If I order you to do something, anything, what will you do?"

"Whatever you say, Mr. Corwin, I'll do it. You just leave me alone."

"All right, Tony. I want the truth from Vollmer here. Don't kill him but if he doesn't answer my questions, beat him until he's almost dead."

Tony looked unhappy but limbered his arms and stood ready.

"Now. Who is the other man called Alex, Vollmer? Give me his name."

Vollmer opened his mouth. It fell closed again.

"Tony," said Corwin.

Vollmer ran but Tony caught him, swung him around and walloped him in the face, two terrible blows. He fell and lay there whimpering and bloody.

Corwin approached and looked down. In that moment he felt like a man without a soul. "Finish him, Tony," he said.

Tony got Vollmer by the shirt, hauled him up and drew back his fist.

"Wait, wait!" screamed Vollmer. "It was Warren. Warren Grimm!"

"Hold it, Tony. Which one of you killed Julie Steadman?"

"He did. He did!"

"You had nothing to do with it?"

"No. Nothing."

"Get ready, Tony. You had nothing at all to do with it?"

"I—" He looked at Tony's great fist poised. "I was there. I mean, I was with him, but I didn't do it."

"But you killed Gordon Steadman, didn't you?"

"No, no! That was Grimm again. He killed—oh, God, he killed them both." Vollmer began to sob.

126

"Just hold him, Tony. You have an outside line here?"

"Over there on the table, Mr. Corwin."

Corwin saw the phone, crossed. He held the phone to the light, remembered the number, dialed.

"Floyd," he said. "I'm at the Vollmers' place. In the apartment over the garage. I've got Matt Vollmer here. And Tony, the chauffeur. Vollmer will swear that Warren Grimm did the killings. Vollmer was there. Come over and pick up these two, then I'll get Grimm.

"And, Floyd, I'm sick. There's something gone wrong inside me. I think there's going to be one more killing tonight."

He hung up.

Chapter 14

He saw the lights coming up the road and knew it was Whitlock. It had taken a long time and he had marched Tony and Vollmer down the drive ahead of him and had made Tony open the gate to let them out. He stood there waiting with the gun at their backs.

He was, in a dazed sort of way, surprised to see that it was a police car and belonged to the sheriff's department. The car pulled up sharply and Whitlock climbed out of the back. When the door opened he could see, vaguely, the forms of two other men in back, two in front.

"You all right?" said Whitlock. In the half-light his face was exceedingly drawn and stern.

"I may never be all right, Floyd. Who've you got there?"

"The sheriff and a couple of his boys. I phoned him."

"Good. Then take these two in and throw the key away. Vollmer's at least an accomplice. Tony-boy here fixed that fender on the convertible and took me for a ride in the woods with Vollmer and Grimm."

"They do this to your face, Todd?"

127

"Tony. But get a look at *him.*"

"I'll take the gun now, Todd. You won't need it."

"That's right. I won't. Here, take two while you're at it." He passed them over. "You know where Grimm lives?"

"I know."

"Just give me the address, Floyd. Hurry, goddamn it! Just give me the address." He knew that his voice sounded odd, but couldn't control it.

"You *are* sick," said Whitlock gravely.

"Oh, screw that. Screw it! Just give me that address."

"It won't be necessary," said Whitlock.

Corwin grabbed Whitlock by the lapels and pulled him close. "Why, goddamn it! Why won't it be necessary?"

"Because," said Whitlock, "we picked him up. Warren Grimm is right there in the back of the car."

He shoved Whitlock and began to run. But they saw it coming and jumped out. It took three of them to hold him. They had his arms pinned behind him. But even so he pulled them to the back window and looked in.

Grimm was handcuffed to a deputy. He had on a dark sport shirt and dark trousers. He looked neat and un-ruffled. With his free hand he ran a comb through the long blond strands of his hair. His pale face looked com-posed, a cigarette dangled from a corner of his mouth. He put the comb away and took the cigarette from his lips.

"Hiya, Corwin," he said. "Told you I'd make news one day. Forgot to tell you how."

There was smug pleasure in his eyes and the trace of a smile drifted across his face.

Corwin strained against the hands that held him, worked his mouth, leaned in the window and spat in Grimm's face.

Lights glared overhead. Smoke filled the sheriff's office. Everyone stopped talking and there was a moment of immense silence as Warren Grimm took the microphone in his hand, crossed his legs comfortably and looked up at the assemblage.

Sheriff Gifford was behind the desk upon which sat the tape recorder. Next to Grimm an officer stood at ease, fingering his holster. The others—Corwin, Whitlock, the deputy sheriff, Matt Vollmer and Tony sat in a semi-circle around the desk. Another officer stood over by the door.

"Now, this will be informal," said Gifford. "We'll take a full written confession in the morning. Vollmer, if you have anything important to add to the facts you gave us earlier speak up." The sheriff paused, turned a long steady gaze on Corwin. "I realize how this will affect you, Corwin. And I'm sorry, of course. But I want to make it plain from the beginning that though you have every right to be here under the circumstances, I would prefer that you remain silent at this time, keep your seat—and your control." He smiled sadly. "Otherwise you'll have to leave. If you don't think you have hold of yourself, say so now."

"I'm all right," said Corwin. Suddenly he was tired. The surge of anger that was like physical pain had gone out of him and he was left with a bottomless disgust. He wanted to see it to the end and then get up in the skies above it all and come down in another world. His own.

The sheriff's jaw rocked. He looked Grimm up and down with infinite contempt and said, "In your own words, Grimm. There'll be questions at another time. Go ahead."

The officer beside Grimm reached over and cut in the recorder. The wheels spun with a faint whispering. Grimm pulled at his trousers, looked over the faces patronizingly, as if about to accept tribute for a lifetime's accomplishment.

"I killed them both," he said and paused dramatically. "All the plans were mine. Matt Vollmer is an idiot, a baby. He came along for the ride and got sucked under the wheels."

"He's a crazy psychopath," said Vollmer, close to tears. "He enjoyed it. Every bit of it. Like a play on a stage with him in the lead. Oh, God, God, God!" He covered his face with his hands.

Grimm smiled indulgently and went on. "It got started because I wanted to have a little fun with Julie Steadman. I was bored and she happened to get under my skin. Gordon Steadman was just a jerk who was in the way and I can tell you about him in one minute flat.

"I never meant to kill him. It was his own fault. He fixed it so I had to. I knew he was getting close and was

129

going to make trouble and wouldn't leave town. Throughout the whole deal, Matt knew everything that was happening inside the police department and out. His Old Man would tell him and he would pass it on to me. Mr. Vollmer didn't want to cover for me but when Matt confessed he was along the night Julie Steadman was killed, Vollmer didn't have a choice. The Old Man may have guessed, but he never knew for sure how Gordon Steadman got it.

"When I heard that Steadman wouldn't leave town, was threatening to make trouble, I got hold of Matt and we went to Steadman's house to beat him up and convince him. The back door had a simple lock and I had a passkey to open it. We went in, wearing masks. I had a gun. We found Steadman in the bedroom. I was giving him a little scare talk first when suddenly he reached over and pulled down my mask.

"I stood there thinking a few seconds. Then I put the gun up to his temple and shot him. I wiped off the gun and made it look like suicide. Matt was no help at all. He cried like a damn hysterical girl. But he was in just as deep and he knew it. Then Corwin came along to complicate the mess and I dreamed up an idea to have Matt kill him with one of the old man's rifles and make it look like an accident. But I should have known that Matt would chicken out at the last minute. And now, gentlemen, try not to go to sleep. Because I'm coming to the good part. Julie Steadman."

Grimm put the microphone in his lap, found cigarettes in his pocket and asked for a light. He got it from the officer next to him and after puffing calmly a moment, set the cigarette in a tray on the desk and again picked up the microphone.

"I saw Julie Steadman for the first time in the personnel office of the *News*. I was in there talking to Alice Troxel. She's a kind of Girl Friday to Frank McClure who runs personnel. I had the hots for Alice and wanted to date her that night. She was busy. But compared to Julie Steadman, Alice didn't bother me at all. The minute she walked in, this Julie, she got glued in my mind like a picture I saw in one of those pornographic books that cost a hundred a copy. She wasn't well dressed or anything, kind of shabby in fact. Didn't matter. The more I looked at her, the more it seemed to me she wasn't wearing any clothes at all.

"Not a big girl. Almost tiny. Little flower of a face with wide doe eyes, pouty mouth and, for a little bitch, the goddamndest cans you ever saw."

Grimm smirked, everyone stirred uncomfortably and Corwin squeezed the arms of his chair.

"I didn't know who she was and I didn't care. I wanted her and I'm used to getting what I want, one way or another. So when I saw that Alice was giving her the no-jobs-today brush, I just waited until she left and followed her. Outside the office I caught up with her and I told her I happened to overhear and maybe I could help. She was all smiles and gratitude.

"I remembered that I had seen Matt go upstairs to his Old Man's office, probably for a touch. It gave me an idea and I told the Steadman doll to sit down and wait until I could see the right people. I went to my desk and watched until Matt came down in a few minutes. I grabbed him at the elevator. He said okay, he would speak to the Old Man that night. I said no, now! Because I had this kitty on the string and didn't wanna let go. Matt gave me a hard time but I always got my way with him and in the end I introduced him to this Julie and he took her name up to A. V. There was some more fooling around and red tape, but she got a job in circulation.

"She had a big-hero grin on her face for me and I cashed in on it by asking her downstairs for coffee. That was when she told me she was married and her husband was in the sub service. He was way out somewhere in the North Atlantic and she didn't know when he'd be back.

"Well, right away I figured her to be restless for a little man-type excitement. So when we left the coffee shop I asked her where she was going next. She said home. She had a car but didn't like to drive in city traffic so she had taken the bus. I said I was going her way and offered her a ride.

"I took one of the *News* radio cars that I drive on assignment and pretended I had to make a stop over by the beach. I just went into a building over there and stayed a couple of minutes. Then I took her down a lonely road to the ocean. She didn't seem to have much sense of direction and didn't catch on until she saw it was a dead end. Then she said, 'Where are you going?' She sounded nervous. 'Must have turned on the wrong road,' I told her. 'Pretty day, though. Might as well look at the water while we're here.'

"She gave me a funny look but didn't say anything until I parked and made a pass. 'Listen,' she said, cold as dry ice, 'you start this car, little man, and take me home right this minute and I might forget to tell my husband.' I just laughed at her and tried again. She pushed me away.

" 'Let me tell you something, little boy,' she said. 'If I were going to cheat on my husband, which I am not, I would pick myself a man, not a pasty juvenile with a pretty face, dirty eyes and a mind like a sewer. Are you sure you're looking for a woman or are you trying to prove to yourself that you would know what to do with one?'

"Well, she had come pretty close to some truth about me which I had been keeping from myself for a long time. I was so angry I wanted to hit her. And at the same time I had to have her all the more. But I started the car and drove her home. We didn't say another word to each other and when we got to the house, she just jumped out and ran inside.

"I tried to kick her out of my head but she wouldn't leave. She hung around all day. I felt as if she had exposed me to myself, left me naked in the mirror of my mind. I hated her. And at the same time I wanted her more than any woman I ever met. I began to think. I began to scheme. I have a very clever mind and a fantastic imagination. I came up with something foolproof. A brilliant idea. It was only a matter of timing.

"I knew she was going to the movies because in the coffee shop I had asked her what she did with her evenings. And she said she lived a very dull existence while her husband was gone. That night, for instance, she was going to a show and it was the most exciting thing she ever did.

"In the afternoon I bought a .38 at a shop where I had a friend who was willing to keep his mouth shut about the sale, for a price. Then I went over to see Matt and told him the plan. He didn't like it but I convinced him it was all in fun and no one would get hurt by it. Besides, I know some things about Matt he would like to have kept quiet. I mentioned them casually and he changed his attitude."

Grimm looked over at Matt Vollmer and again he smirked.

"Matt was to pretend that he wasn't going to see me because I had to work. He faked various other plans, finally discarded them all and pretended to go to bed. Then he snuck out with the red Caddy convertible and met me in the theater parking lot.

"Meanwhile, I had waited in my own car outside Julie Steadman's house to see what time she left. I saw her take a bus around eight and I followed. She went into the Southside Theater. She was in time for the last show which the box office told me broke a few minutes after eleven."

Grimm took the cigarette from the tray, sucked in smoke and went on.

"I met Matt and we sat in the car and had some slugs from a bottle, waiting. It was dark and no one saw us. We discussed the plan and, after a few drinks, being a lecherous type, the idea began to seem rather appealing to Matt, too. Both of us had tried about everything there was to do in this goddamn world. We both had enough dough to get any kind of kick you can name and we were bored with all the usual crappy amusements. This was a new thrill.

"Just before eleven we parked near the show and watched. When Julie Steadman came out she started walking toward the bus stop a couple of blocks away on a pretty dark street. We timed it to arrive there just as she did. Matt stopped and leaned out. 'Mrs. Steadman,' he called, 'Oh, Mrs. Steadman!'

"I heard her approach but I didn't see her. Because by this time I was on the floor in back, holding the gun and wearing a mask over my face. 'It's Matt Vollmer, Mrs. Steadman!' said Matt. 'You remember, I met you this morning. My father owns the *News*.' Well, she was very polite. You could almost hear the bow in her voice. And when Matt said he was just coming from the movie himself and would take her home, she hopped right in."

"I let a few blocks go by and then I raised up and stuck the gun right at Matt's head. 'This is a stick-up, Mac,' I

133

said in a hard voice much different from my own. 'Next time you park in a dark lot, stupid, you better lock your car. Now drive where I tell you.'

"Julie Steadman got one look at the gun and me in the mask and she was one scared kitty. She chewed her lip and didn't say a word. I gave Matt directions. A pre-arranged, god-forsaken place off a country road by a stream. There's a little rotting shack and nothing else but trees. I told him to stop near the shack. Then I made them both give me their money. Matt protested, talked hard, threatened, but, as planned, got very quiet and obedient when I told him to do as he was told or I'd shoot them both.

"And then I ordered her to strip her clothes off. All but her shoes and stockings. And when she wouldn't, I ordered Matt to help her. Matt said I was a maniac and she'd better not argue with me. She began to cry, but she obeyed, down to the last. Jesus God, what a body! Matt's eyes were big as golf balls. I told him to hand over the car keys and wait there or get shot. He gave me the keys and then I walked her to the shack.

"I put the gun in my pocket and I grabbed her. I tried to kiss her but she fought like a goddamn wildcat. So I got her by the hair and held her head still until I could clamp my mouth down on hers. Then she pretended to like it and to play along, but the little bitch bit my tongue. I damn near broke her arm and she let go in a hurry. I had the arm shoved up in back of her and every time she tried to scratch or kick me, I put on the pressure.

"After that she wasn't much trouble. I kissed her on the neck, shoulders, all over, while I squeezed one of those beautiful big knockers. Oh, Christ, what a woman! And all she did was whimper and beg me to stop. Oh, man, that pleading bit was just music to me. It boiled me that much hotter and I was out of my mind to have her.

"So I shoved her down on her back and I got one hand around her throat and I told her if she didn't play I'd choke the life out of her. She went limp and then I gave the bitch what she really wanted from me all the time. And the more she cried, the more I—"

Corwin hurled himself across the room and in a red frenzy, hammered his fist into Warren Grimm's face.

LAMENT FOR JULIE

Grimm went over backwards, crashing with his chair to the floor. Corwin was bent above him, raising his fist, when two of the guards pulled him off and forced him back to his seat.

Wiping a trickle of blood from his mouth, Grimm got slowly to his feet. No one bothered to help him, though a guard had righted his chair. And now he sat waiting, the small twisted smile returning to his face.

"Corwin," said Gifford sternly. "You move an inch from that chair again and I'll throw you out myself!" But as he turned to Grimm, the sheriff's tongue probed, made a lump in his cheek. It was like a wink. "All right, Grimm, get on with it," he said disgustedly.

Grimm made a final swipe at his bleeding mouth and continued.

"We came back and she got dressed, blubbering, 'If you'll let us go without hurting us, I'll never tell.' And I said, 'Fair enough, lady. Don't tell, but remember you had a *man*.' I couldn't help adding that. She was working on some buttons and she became very still and quiet. 'You're not a bad sort, after all,' she said. She took my hand and gave it a little squeeze. I felt her fingers touching my wrist and I was surprised. She dropped my hand. 'Oh, you're really a very nice young man,' she said. 'And I know who you are. I remember that watchband. Leather and gold. Very unusual. And something you said. About being a man. Why, you're Warren Grimm. And when I get to town, they'll put you behind bars where all filthy insane animals belong. I'll see to that. They might even have a lynch mob before I get through with you.'

"I tried to bluff her with a line about never hearing of anyone by the name of Warren Grimm but I'd just as soon have it pinned on him as anyone. She just laughed in a bitter nasty way. Then she reached up and gave me a terrible slap. With that she walked off toward the road and I stood there stunned, powerless to stop her.

"We talked about it after she was gone. Matt was sick with fear. I was in a daze. I got behind the wheel, reached in my pocket and found the keys. I stared at them, put them in the switch. 'I'll drive,' I said.

"She was walking along the road towards town, half running, really. She looked back and saw us make the

135

turn, then ran on. We passed her, gathering speed. We left her far behind. I began to feel better. The night air whipping over me and all that power under me gave me a feeling of calm. Cool deadly calm. My mind began to function. I braked and turned around.

" 'Where you going?' Matt said. 'Better pick her up and take her home,' I answered. He didn't say anything but, 'Oh, God,' over and over. I had the high beams on and I must have seen her in the headlights a long way off. I gunned up to about sixty. She saw us, thought it was someone else and got out in the middle of the road, waving frantically.

"I felt good now. I felt like a man again. I never felt better. Life had been dull. Life had been stale. And this had been a night of kicks like no other I could remember. With one more thrill to come, the daddy of them all.

"This puny little fluff in the middle of the road had made me feel weak and unimportant. She was going to send me to jail. Mobs were going to lynch me. I wanted to laugh out loud. And then she was just a few yards off and I turned the wheel as if I would pass her. But at the last second I swung in sharply. She tried to leap back. But I caught her with the right fender. Her mouth was open for a scream that never came.

"There was a pulpy thud and she went sailing. Like a limp doll with arms beating the air, she went flinging off into the night. Gone. Gone. And I picked up speed, feeling good. That was when I felt the best. Like a man again. More than a man." He paused and looked around the room. "I was a god."

"I *was* God."

Corwin did not remember just what happened after that. Except that someone had him in a hammerlock. And then they were dragging him out to the hall and quieting him. And now he came out of the john from being sick and was taking deep gulps of air. Next to him, in the hall, Whitlock stood talking with the sheriff when Austin Vollmer came bursting in the front door, trailed by Gail Vollmer.

Vollmer had hold of the sheriff's arm, swinging him

around. "What the goddamn hell, Gifford," he said. "Someone called and said you've got my son down here under arrest. Who the hell do you think you are, Gifford? You let that boy go. Now! Hear me?"

The sheriff looked at him. Impassively. As if he were a minor disturbance, a small noise in a night of great thunder. He took the hand away from his arm. "You'll get plenty of chance to see your boy, Vollmer," he said. "Until you can make bail I might let you share the same cell. Now keep your mouth shut and come with me."

"Go with you? Keep my mouth shut?" Vollmer thrust his face close to the sheriff's. "Listen, Gifford, don't start sounding official with me. Don't you give *me* orders. You're just a bag of straw, a dummy with a badge. I stuffed you, I pumped you up. And I can let the air out of you with one little prick, just a phone call. Don't you forget it!"

Gifford placed a big hand on Vollmer's chest and shoved him off contemptuously. "You'll have a chance to make that call. Every prisoner gets one call, even a Vollmer. You can call the White House if you like. Nothing's gonna help you, anyway. Just remember, Vollmer, that I was elected to this office and up to the last minute before my term ends, I still run this show. And I'm gonna lock you up and throw away the key until a jury decides what to do with you."

"Why, you stupid sonofabitch," said Vollmer, "you'll answer to the governor himself in the morning! Now, I'm leaving here and don't you dare try to stop me."

He turned, took two strides and Whitlock stepped in front of him, hard-put to contain the grin tugging at the corners of his mouth.

"Going someplace, Austin?" he said. "Take one more pace and you'll be resisting arrest. In a case like that, I'd just have to climb all over you so you wouldn't get away. Perfectly legal, you know."

Vollmer chewed on his cigar, studying the bulk of Whitlock, the first hint of fear weakening the set of his jaw. He backed, caught sight of Corwin, suddenly aimed an accusing finger.

"You!" he said. "You brought all this. This was a quiet peaceful town, everybody minding their own business until you came and stirred up trouble with your goddamn lies."

"That's right," said Corwin. "Everybody minding their own business at your command. That's exactly why I came, Vollmer."

"You'll wish you hadn't, boy. I'll be out of here in an hour and by God, you'll wish you hadn't ever come to this town. I'll find you wherever you are and then I'll show you how we handle your kind."

"You do that," said Corwin quietly. "I just hope you'll do that, Vollmer. I'll be waiting."

"I wouldn't hold my breath," said Gifford. "You'll have a long wait for this baby. Okay, Whitlock, he's all yours. Don't bruise 'im any more than you have to. Just get 'im to that cell."

"Hell," said Whitlock, "you'll hardly see a mark on 'im." He shoved Vollmer ahead of him along the corridor, the sheriff following just behind.

Gail looked after them, biting her lip.

"I don't feel sorry for him in the least," she said. "I should be glad. I've hated him a long time. But I don't feel anything at all."

"I need air," said Corwin. "Not this kind, either."

He went to the door. She followed him out into the night and they began to walk.

"Where will you go now?" she said.

"To the airport."

"I want to go with you."

"You wouldn't like me. I'd be miserable company. Don't misunderstand, Gail. But you'd better not."

"All right."

They reached the Buick, he opened the door and got behind the wheel. She came around and stood by his window. "I don't suppose you'll ever come and visit me," she said.

"No," he said. "I'll never be back." He started the motor. "But give me a little space and a little time and I might send you a plane ticket."

"One way?"

He nodded. "One way."

For a long moment he studied her face, wanting to hold the memory of a new depth and softness he saw etched there in lines of pain and sadness. In that brief violent space of time, Gail had mellowed and ripened, had found herself. And yet her basic goodness had always been visible just beneath the surface. It was only that in his torment, in the confusion of loyalties, he was unable to see.

Suddenly he felt cast adrift from old loyalties, his terrible obligation to the Steadmans. And knew, especially, his first freedom from the clutch of Julie, holding tight, crying vengeance, even from the grave. And in a flash of insight, Corwin saw that he was also free to love again. For in all the binding secret years of Julie there had been no room in him to love anyone else. Until now. Until Gail.

"I'll miss you," she said. "Oh, how I'll miss you!"

"Not for long," he answered, touching her cheek. "I won't keep you waiting, baby. Not for long."

She leaned in and kissed him. He gave himself to the kiss. Hungrily but without violence. Passionately but without the need to hurt. Then he released her and drove away.

In the mirror he saw her sad little wave, still felt the sweet cling of her mouth. And knew it would be only a little while.

Then he turned a corner.

And she was gone.

THE END